WITCHES OF THE BIG EASY, BOOK ONE

HEXXED

SHANNON WEST

Hexxed

Copyright © 2019 Shannon West

Published by Painted Hearts Publishing

About the Book You Have Purchased

Hexxed

Copyright © 2019 Shannon West

ISBN 13: 9781686963902

Author: Shannon West
Editor: Ashley Kain
Proofreader: Kira Plotts
All cover art and logo copyright © 2019 by Painted Hearts
Publishing
Cover Design by E Keith

Foreword

Bram Stoker said, "There are things which we cannot understand, and yet which are; that some people see that others cannot." Do you believe in such things as spirits and witches? Vampires and demons? Is it possible these things exist?

Medieval maps often pointed out places where there was danger from things we couldn't always see—until it was too late. They used illustrations of dragons, sea monsters and other mythological creatures to point out places where such danger was thought to exist. HC SVNT DRACONES or HERE BE DRAGONS was code for this, a metaphor, in a way, for the paranormal or magical creatures thought to roam in certain places. Most of the time, the maps were wrong and the edges of the map simply showed unknown or uncharted territory. But sometimes, the old mapmakers got it right.

Portals have always existed in our world. Entrances, like cracks in a wall, for the unknown to come through. Most often these cracks appear in places where the wall is already thin between this world and others. The city of New Orleans has always been such a place.

And where these creatures exist, there must be lawmakers and peacekeepers. Those who will make sure the evil doesn't take over and blot out all the good. Those who will protect the innocents of this world and keep humans from knowing about what coexists with them in this world. The *législateurs*, a group of powerful witches, also known as *Les Batons*, perform this duty for New Orleans, for both the living and the undead, both by day and after dark in the city known as The Big Easy.

"We all start out knowing magic.

We are born with whirlwinds, forest fires, and comets

inside us."

— John McCammon

Chapter One

Dominic Gaudet

"Wait here for me," I told my driver as he pulled up to the entrance of Hotel Hypnotiq, the newest of my family's line of luxury boutique hotels. "I'll only be a minute, and you can drive me over to Ravenwood so I can murder Thibeau Delessard."

The black storm clouds gathering over the elegant old New Orleans Garden District matched my mood perfectly as I got out, slamming the car door behind me. I burst through the front doors of the hotel, not stopping to speak to the doorman who came rushing over, and sparing only the briefest of nods to the young bellman. I didn't return any of the greetings of the shocked staff members at the front desk either as they watched me sweep through the lobby with startled eyes. I no doubt looked like I wanted to commit murder—which I did—just not anybody here at the hotel. My potential victim was across town at his family estate, probably thinking up more ways to ruin my life.

The people manning the desk looked everywhere but directly at me. One of them jerked his thumb quickly over his shoulder when I ground out the words, "Where's my brother?"

Gabriel came out from the back, his welcoming smile freezing when he saw me. "Nic, what are you doing here? Is something wrong?"

"You might say that," I replied, maybe a little too loud. Okay, no maybe about it. It was at least loud enough that my younger brother glanced at the handful of guests milling around the lobby, a man and woman coming out of the breakfast room and a couple of older women looking at brochures by the desk. The man and woman were darting nervous glances at us and the old ladies were whispering behind their hands. No doubt they all thought they were in the middle of some delicious family drama. Or maybe they were wondering if they should call the cops.

We *were* the cops, actually, though they had no way of knowing that. My brother and I were *législateurs*, the governing body of all the magic practitioners and supernatural beings in this part of the world, both the living and the undead. Those shadowy figures you catch out of the corner of your eye after dark, particularly in a city like the Big Easy, where the veil between the past and present, the living and the dead felt very thin. We made sure that no one practiced acts of dark magic of any kind on innocents. We considered such acts to be a grievous crime and we dealt with them swiftly and with extreme prejudice.

Old Abel Delessard had been a witch, not a practitioner of dark magic—or at least, we hadn't been able to catch him at it. Still, he was a strong and powerful practitioner, and since he'd been murdered in his own home less than a week ago, we needed to know who had killed him and why. And on a more personal note, I needed to find out why his grandson Thibeau Delessard had not only failed to report Abel's murder to the *législateurs*—a huge mistake and one he had to answer for—but had also made an outrageous accusation to the police against me and my family.

Gabriel gave the guests in the lobby a practiced smile, though he glanced at me nervously, taking my arm to draw me back into his office and close the door behind us. His blue eyes were full of concern.

"Calm down, Nic. Whatever it is can be handled. My God, what are you so pissed off about?"

"Oh, do I seem pissed off?" I said, pacing around his office, still way too angry to take a seat. "Really? Do you have any idea who came to my office this morning?"

"Your office in New York? No," he said, his eyes narrowing. "Who?"

"A New York City homicide detective, Gabriel. A goddamn New York City homicide detective came to my office to speak to me this morning. He said he was making inquiries on behalf of the Jefferson Parrish PD regarding Abel Delessard's untimely demise. It seems old Abel shuffled off this mortal coil not quite a week ago—were you fucking aware of that fact?"

"Well, yes, I did hear about it, but I had no idea the police were involved."

I cast a gimlet eye at him. "And it never occurred to you to *tell me* the old sonofabitch was dead?"

"I was going to, Nic, but we've been so busy—the hotel has been full and we've had two wedding receptions in the garden just in the past week. Business is booming, as a matter of fact, and to tell you the truth, I didn't think Abel's death was that much of a surprise. The man was in his late eighties and in poor health, wasn't he?"

"The mortal enemy of our family, the *de facto* owner of the De Lys blood diamond is murdered in his own basement and you didn't think it was important enough to give me a call?"

"*M-murdered?*" Gabriel flushed, stumbling over the word. He looked stunned as I flopped down in a chair near the desk. I was suddenly exhausted as some of the adrenalin that had been fueling me since I left New York began to drain away. It left me feeling hot and bothered and not in a good way.

"But I had no idea! Why on earth weren't the *Législateurs* notified?"

"Good question," I replied grimly. "I intend to find out."

I would relish a chance to take my anger out on someone from that family and teach them proper law. Preferably Thibeau Delessard. "That sonofabitch Thibeau sent the police to see *me*. Told them there was 'bad blood' between our two families, and he strongly suspected that I had something to do with the murder." I hit the arm of my chair with my fist. "Bad blood, my ass! There's going to be some bad blood, all right, and all of it *his*! Has he forgotten we're *Législateurs*? And that any kind of unnatural death of a practitioner has to be reported to us immediately! If he has, I'm going to give him a strong reminder."

4

"The police came to talk to you *in New York*? But you weren't anywhere near New Orleans when Abel died." He glanced at me sharply. "Were you?"

"Of course, I wasn't, damn it! And I pointed that out to the homicide detective. He asked a few more questions, and thank God I had an airtight alibi, so he left. But not before implying that I might have hired someone to do my dirty work for me and telling me that either he or the detectives from Jefferson Parrish might want to speak to me again in the near future so I should '*keep myself available.' Fils de pute.*"

"But nothing can come of it, surely! You're innocent! You *are* innocent, Nic, aren't you? I mean, you didn't do anything to him, did you?"

I glared at him in response.

"Well, I know Abel Delessard has been involved or at least on the fringes of some shady stuff over the years. Nothing that we could prove, but…anyway, you said you have an airtight alibi and I'm sure you called our lawyers. We don't need any trouble from the police."

"Obviously not. And yes, I called the lawyers and the others. It was the first thing I did. Right after booking my flight to New Orleans."

"You didn't call me."

"No, I didn't call you, because I was going to see you as soon as I landed."

"But Nic, surely that wasn't necessary. I can assure you that I can handle the investigation into Abel's death."

I waved his concerns away and shook my head. "I know you can, Gabriel. But this one is personal for me. I'm sure you understand why."

"Because of Thibeau."

"I want to wrap my hands around his throat and watch him squirm. That lying *putain!*"

"Don't sugarcoat it, Nic. Tell me how you really feel about him." Gabriel smirked down at me, and I felt a little better, like I always did in the company of my favorite younger brother. I was still going to kill Thibeau—probably—but I did feel better. Thibeau Delessard and I had a history, one I'd been trying desperately for the past two years to forget. Hard to believe it had been that long since I'd seen him, but he'd effectively shut down every attempt I'd made to contact him, every chance I gave him to explain, refusing to take my calls, ignoring all the emails and texts I'd sent him. Even getting a damn restraining order against me when I kept trying to contact him. After two years of it, I'd finally given up. Well, mostly.

"I came to get the key to the house on Dauphine Street."

"To get...? Are you staying there? But you can stay here with me. We have a suite available."

"I appreciate the offer, but I may need privacy for an investigation, and Dauphine Street is perfect for that. If anyone's looking for me or Taylor, that's where we'll be until we leave to go back to New York." I started toward the door and stopped. "Except for Mother. If she calls you looking for me, tell her you have no idea where I am."

"Are you fighting with her again?"

"There is no 'again,' Gabriel. That would imply we've stopped at some point. And to be fighting, I'd have to be speaking to her, and I avoid that at all costs. No, nothing new, but we had to have the talk again about her interference in my affairs, and now she's playing the martyr. I don't have time for it, and God knows I don't have the patience."

"Okay. If she calls, I'll tell her I haven't seen you. How long are you planning on staying?"

"It depends on whether or not things go the way I hope they will. I plan to go over to their home in an official capacity and impress upon that family the importance of following practitioner law. Not to mention *not* bringing my name or my family's name up to any police officer at any time in the future. If I have to wring Thibeau Delessard's little neck or beat some sense into him to make that happen, so be it. Now give me the key and I'll be on my way."

He opened his desk drawer and pulled out the key to the small cottage in the French Quarter that had belonged to our family since they first arrived in America and settled in New Orleans in the late 1800s. I'd recently had it renovated and hadn't had a chance to get back down here to inspect the changes. This would give me that opportunity. Gabriel passed the key across the desk to me. "Here it is. But Nic, don't do anything you'll regret. You're not really going to..."

"Maybe not. Probably not. Depends on how much he runs that little mouth of his. Or how much he tries to. I brought a few gags

7

with his name on them, not to mention my favorite flogger. The problem is he'd like that too much. You should have seen the look on the face of the Homeland security guard at the airport when she went through my bags. One way or another, though, I'm going to teach that little bastard a lesson he won't soon forget." I stood up and grinned at him. "*Bon soir*, little brother. I'm off to Ravenwood to catch a rat."

XXXX

Thibeau Delessard

I hate funerals. Not that they're anybody's idea of a good time, but I had a particular aversion to them, and I usually made some patently flimsy excuse to get out of going to one. But when the guest of honor was your own grandfather, there really wasn't any way to get out of it gracefully.

My grandfather had been a major force in my life, and he had raised me and my siblings after our parents had been killed in a car accident when I was eight years old. My sister Sophie was four and Rafe had been little more than a baby. Abel Delessard was a hard man. To three young children, devastated over the sudden loss of their parents, he hadn't been a soft place to land. At the ripe old age of eight, I had become the caretaker of the little ones, letting both of them crawl in bed with me at night until the old man found out about it and put a stop to it.

Odd how those memories still lingered when so many others had fled. I still remembered the night he came in and found Rafe beside me in bed. He and I shared a bedroom and Rafe had learned to climb out of his crib and get in the bed with me. That night, I'd been rubbing his back the way I'd seen our mama do to settle him down. I think I was singing one of the songs she sang, though I didn't really know the words. Funny that I can still remember her singing to us, but I can't remember her face anymore. That was one of the memories burned away, right along with my magic.

Abel wasn't necessarily a cruel man, but he had a strict code of conduct for everyone in his life—a firm grasp of how things *should* be according to the gospel of Abel. The man was a little like a Fundamentalist preacher in that respect. He had snatched Rafe up that night and carried him back over to his crib, throwing him roughly down inside it. Rafe had shrieked his fright and stood back up, reaching his arms out for me, and my grandfather had backhanded him. He'd only hit him once, but Rafe hadn't been quite two years old.

When I jumped out of bed with my fists clenched and called Abel a name I'd heard our father use once when someone cut him off in traffic, the old man had used his magic to hurl me across the room. I suppose he thought it was his duty and responsibility to make us into strong men and to keep us all on the straight and narrow. Some people might find that odd, considering he was also one of the most powerful witches in North America.

Witchcraft was our family business, you might say, and had been since probably the late Middle Ages, when the first Delessard studied alchemy under the old masters themselves. We had a portrait of Henri Delessard hanging over our fireplace in the library. He wasn't a handsome or charismatic figure, but he was a secret practitioner of strong magic and a witch who used his powers only for good.

My ancestors like old Henri were rich, and thus had tremendous advantage and privilege. Yet even they had to be extremely careful. Magic has always been secret, especially in the Middle Ages, where innocents were regularly tortured and burned at the stake, most times simply for being old, poor and eccentric. None of my ancestors were ever put to death by the authorities, although, as with any family, they had suffered various tragedies over the centuries. Some said it was because of an old family curse.

"Thibeau!" My brother Rafe's voice drifted out of the hallway into my room. My name was another "gift" from Abel, as my father was a Junior. When I was born, Thibaut Abel Delessard had insisted on there being a Third. Abel hated the spelling of my name though, and said he had named my father "Thib*aut*," with that particular spelling, after himself, and because it was a fine old Cajun name to be proud of. My mother had tried softening the spelling a little so I wouldn't have such a hard a time in school, but it hadn't worked.

After years of the other kids calling me "Thigh Bo" in practically every school I ever went to—it was actually pronounced *Tee-Bo*—my name had become just another cross I had to bear. Like being gay in the South or like not telling anyone that I came from a long line of witches.

"In here," I called out, and Rafe pushed open the door and came in.

"*Ça va*, bro? Don't you want something to eat? Camille and her friends brought in like a ton of food."

Camille Dubois was our elderly cook and housekeeper, and she had been around forever, or as far back as I could remember anyway. She lived in a house on the Ravenwood grounds, along with her son, Emmanuel, whom Abel employed as our gardener and general handyman.

Camille had been appalled at the lack of casserole dishes brought to the house after my grandfather's death. She was a southerner and Cajun and therefore used to friends and relatives bringing in an endless array of beans and rice, cakes and pies and pots of étouffée and gumbo for the bereaved family members to try and consume after the funeral of one of their loved ones. When none had been forthcoming from *our* relatives—who consisted of one elderly aunt and a few cousins, who all lived in Florida, as I tried to explain to her—she had taken the problem to her church and she and the other good ladies of the Emmanuel Methodist Episcopal Church had been lugging food into the house all morning long.

"I couldn't eat any more if I tried. Be sure Camille gets the names of the people who brought us all the food, though. Even if we won't be able to eat it all, it was still a really nice gesture. We should send thank you notes to them."

"I'll help," he said, plopping down beside me on the couch. "With the eating, that is. Sophie has a better handwriting than I do, so she can do the notes. Camille said any food left over can be frozen. Not that I plan on letting the bread pudding and the sweet potato pound cake sit around long enough to need freezing."

I smiled at him and reached over to ruffle his dark hair. "Don't make yourself sick. You're supposed to be too bereaved to eat all that much."

Rafe shrugged and sighed. "Is it bad I'm really not? I did care about him…in a way…"

"Don't worry about it. He was a hard man to love."

His eyes got dark and stormy for a second. "Who do you think killed him, Thibeau? And how did they get in the cellar vault anyway? He always kept the wards in place, didn't he?"

"He did. And I have no idea how anyone got in."

"He *never* forgot. He guarded that cellar so that the only ones the wards *wouldn't* keep out were the family members, and of course, Camille and Emmanuel. I'm still thinking it had to be the Gaudets. No one else would have had the power to breach those wards that way."

As much as it pained me to think it, I was afraid he might be right. The only other practitioners powerful enough or brazen enough to come inside our home or get past the magical wards my grandfather had in place indeed had to have been one of the Gaudets.

The big Gaudet family were all *législateurs*, the governing body that had been in existence since the Middle Ages in Europe, and arrived in New Orleans back in the early 1700s when the place was only a French colony called La Nouvelle-Orléans. At one time our family had been *législateurs* too, but something happened way back that had changed all that and made our families mortal enemies to the Gaudets. I had forgotten exactly what it was.

The *législateurs* dealt not only with high magic but with all types of magic, including voodoo and folk magic, like hoodoo, rootwork and conjure. They policed the witches, and also the undead and other paranormal creatures—those who roamed the shadows in the outskirts of the old city. Usually, you never saw them, and your only awareness of them might be when you felt that little prickle of danger on your skin or when the hair rose on the back of your neck. But it was never a good idea to wander in those areas after dark.

Locally in the magic community, the *législateurs* were known as *les batons*, a name with a Cajun flair. It was given to them as a sign of respect with maybe a touch of spite, in reaction to their practice of carrying wands when they were on duty. The word "*baton*" was pronounced in the Louisiana way, like "*bat*-ahn," with the emphasis on the first syllable. *Les batons*, or the "sticks" may have referred not only to their wands, but also to their strict, stern demeanor when they were intent after some wrongdoer. Most of us were a little afraid of them, though we didn't like to admit it.

Dominic Gaudet headed up the *batons* now, and he and his two brothers, were prominent members of the group. It would be strange indeed for them to have killed Abel, since he wasn't a warlock or a dark magic practitioner. Still, the Gaudet family was our family's greatest enemy, so when the police asked me if my grandfather might have had any enemies, their name sprang to my mind—and my lips—too soon. Once the name slipped out, I couldn't very well pull it back.

The feud between the Delessards and the Gaudets—one that had come down through the centuries—existed even today. If I had ever known the cause of it, like I said, I had no memory of it now. Truthfully, the feud had never mattered much to me, and even less now that Nic Gaudet was out of my life.

Nic was living in New York City now, and a man as gorgeous as he was, as powerful and rich, had undoubtedly moved on with his life long before now and had forgotten I even existed. Despite everything that had happened between us, or maybe because of it, I had a hard time seeing Nic Gaudet as a murderer.

He may have been my family's enemy. My ruination and my torment. The first thought I had in the mornings and the last one I had at night, as well as the only man I would ever love. But he was no murderer. In fact, he was the best man I ever knew.

Yet if it hadn't been a Gaudet, then who? Who could have hated my grandfather enough to come into our home and murder him?

The wards were no longer in place when Rafe found Abel—he had come running into my room that night—or I should say in the wee hours of the morning—in a panic looking for me, and I hadn't felt the wards guarding the door as usual when I rushed into the cellar. Abel was there on the floor in a spreading pool of blood, Even though Abel was dead I could feel the barest trace of them, the remnants, hanging in the air and lingering like a bad odor. But there was also a residue of something else in the room too, when I first went in. This was a smell like rotting leaves, and an oily, humid thickness to the air like in the dog days of summer.

Though my own magic was gone now, I still had an awareness, a sense of when dark magic had been used in an area. But almost as soon as I had noticed the—whatever it was—it was gone again. I'd still stepped back in alarm like I'd stepped on something soft and mushy in the grass.

"We don't know anything for sure," I told Rafe. "We have to let the police handle it from here. I did give Nic Gaudet's name to the detective working the case. He said they'd look into it."

Rafe cast a surprised glance over at me from under those thick eyelashes. "You gave them the name of one of the *batons*? That won't go over too well, to say the least. Won't you be in trouble?"

"Probably. But I was only telling the truth. The Gaudets had a feud with our family, and Nic is the head of the Gaudets. Besides, who else would have had the power to get past those wards?"

He was quiet for a moment, thinking it over. "Still, I think we were supposed to contact the *batons* to report the death before we contacted the police. Abel never followed the law the way he should have, and he never taught much of it to us either. I hope we don't get in too much trouble for it. You know," he said, "maybe now that Abel's gone…we can all finally be happy. I know you suffered the most."

"What are you talking about?"

"Your love life," he said, giving me a jab in the ribs. "Or the lack thereof, I should say. I know how Abel felt about the gay thing. And I know how he was pressuring you to get married and have little Delessard babies. You've been bearing the brunt of that, so I didn't have to."

I gave a heartfelt sigh. "He just had certain beliefs."

"That we both had to suffer for."

Rafe didn't know the half of it, and if I had my way, he never would. I stood up, stretching. "I need to get moving. As for Abel, he thought he was doing the right thing for us, I think. I have to believe that. Not that you've been 'suffering' all that much, anyway. I know all about the clubs and the partying."

"Well, I have to live my life, regardless of what Abel thought. You should come out with me sometime."

"Those clubs are not exactly my scene."

"You know that I'm aware of what that scene is, don't you, Thibeau?"

"I don't do that anymore," I said, shaking my head firmly. "Not for a long time."

"Because of Abel? Or because of Nic Gaudet?" he asked, his oddly colored, blue-green eyes getting stormy again on my account. "He was your…what do you call it? Your Dom, wasn't he?"

"That was a long time ago, and I don't talk about Nic Gaudet. Not ever."

Rafe knew a little of my history, but I had spared him the worst of it, and Abel had hidden the rest very well. If Rafe had known, he would have hated Abel with everything in him. He would have fought for me back when it began and found a way to get himself kicked out of the house, and I didn't want my little brother living on the streets. Or even worse, he might have suffered the same fate I had, so I had kept Abel's secrets close to my chest and kept my mouth shut. The old man was gone now, so there wasn't really any point in rehashing things.

"Abel was…I won't speak ill of the dead. I had to convince myself a while ago that he did what he thought was the right thing for me. He was from a different generation. Had a different belief system."

"I wish you'd tell me about what happened. Sophie and I have been worried about you, and Abel wouldn't tell us where you were for those months you went missing. He didn't…" his eyes went wide and horrified. "God, Thibeau, he didn't put you in one of those religious camps, did he? The ones where they try to pray the gay away?"

It had been so much worse than that, but I'd never tell him the truth, because what would be the point? It was all water under the bridge now, and I'd survived and come out the other side mostly intact. It would only make him think he should have known or should have done something, and he'd simply been too young and powerless to help me. If he'd have even tried, he might have suffered the same fate as I had, and I wouldn't wish that on my worst enemy, let alone my baby brother.

I sighed and stood up. "I really don't want to talk about it. Besides, it's over now. And I need to change clothes and get to the bank before it closes to transfer money from savings into the checking account, unless we want Abel's funeral check to bounce."

"There's this thing called the internet, Beau. Don't know if you've ever heard of it or not."

"Yeah, smartass, I'm aware. But I need to take the death certificate down to the bank anyway, so they can take Abel's name off the account. It won't take long if I can make it before closing time."

A doorbell rang below and I sighed. "What now? I thought all the guests had left."

"Most of them. A few of the church ladies stayed behind to help Camille. I'll go see who it is."

He left and I turned toward my closet to quickly divest myself of my dark suit and tie. I slipped into some soft, well-worn jeans and a sweat shirt instead. I was just changing shoes when Rafe poked his head back in the door.

"I think you better come down, Beau. It's, uh, damn, it's actually Nic Gaudet himself. Speak of the devil, huh? He's here officially, he said, and he asked to see you. Well, all of the family, but you in particular. He said he has questions."

"Damn it! Nic is *here*? In New Orleans?" I stood there thunderstruck for a moment, wishing I could sink through the floor or just somehow disappear. Anything to get out of seeing Nic again. It wasn't that I didn't want to see him, but I wasn't ready. I didn't know if I'd ever be ready. I knew there was no getting out of it now, though, and I cursed my big mouth again. I should never have given the police his name. That had to be why he was here.

I blew out a breath as Rafe watched me carefully. "Should I tell him you can't see anybody right now?"

I gave a short, bitter laugh. "Do you think that would work?"

"No, but it's worth a try."

"It would only make things worse. Is he...did he seem angry?"

"Oh, hell yeah, he's pissed off. He's got some guy with him too. Big dude. His enforcer, I guess—I think he's a *baton* too. And Nic is wearing a big ring with the insignia on it. That means he's the main man now, right? He acts like it. He even made all the old ladies leave, and told Camille to go get Emmanuel. He wants all of us in the parlor, like right now."

The ring he was referring to was a big platinum one that extended all the way to the knuckle. It had the insignia of the *législateurs,* and only the leader wore one. I had to admit I was a little impressed. I'd known Nic was powerful, but it seemed a lot had changed since I'd last seen him.

"I better come down then. And Nic hardly needs an enforcer, as strong as he is. No, we have to talk to him. Just...just give me a minute, okay? Show them to the front parlor and tell him I'll be right down. Oh, and Rafe, be nice, okay? No matter what he says or what his attitude is. I was wrong not to notify the *batons* right away. If I'd been thinking straight, I'd have remembered they had to be told first."

He left and I went to the bathroom to splash some cool water on my face. I combed my hair, too and then put on another shirt from my closet. A blue button up, because Nic always liked me in blue. My hands were shaking as I pulled open the bedroom door and made my way downstairs. I had to pull myself together fast, because I was feeling a little light headed and dizzy. The last thing I needed was to faint dead away at his feet the first time I'd seen him in over two years.

I heard the voices from the front parlor and headed in that direction on shaky legs. Then as I rounded the corner, there he was, Nic Gaudet. He was wearing a dark blue Armani suit, stylishly cut to fit snugly around his slim waist. His thick dark hair was still short on the sides and in the back but longer on top. His eyes were the same striking sapphire blue and framed with those same long, curling lashes. His face was chiseled and perfect—he was, in a word, breathtaking. The first time I'd ever seen him I'd stopped talking in mid-sentence, because I'd thought he was the best-looking thing I'd ever seen. Nothing had changed about that.

He stood up as I entered and took a quick step toward me. I stopped dead still as he came over and got all up in my personal space. I had to tilt my head up to look at him as he frowned down at me. His face was cold and set but his eyes were stormy with some strong emotion.

"Thibeau," he said, in his smooth voice, the tone as rich and dark as molasses. "It's been a while."

"Yes," I said, feeling breathless and struggling even to speak. He didn't move to take the hand I held out to him—just looked down at it instead and his lip curled upward a little.

"You want to shake my hand? Really?"

I pulled it back quickly, feeling stupid. "No, no, I...I'm sorry." I took a step back and looked over at Rafe for help. He came over to take my arm and pull me over to the sofa to sit beside him. I saw that Sophie and her husband Christophe had also been summoned as well and were sitting opposite us. Sophie looked wrecked, her usually bright eyes a little glazed over. The last time I'd seen her she said she and Christophe were heading to their room to rest. Sophie had been the closest of all of us to the old man, and she had taken his death the hardest by far. The doctor had given her a sedative to take and the last time I'd seen her, she had been drooping on Christophe's shoulder. She looked as if she should be in bed right now.

I smiled at her sympathetically and looked up to see Nic watching me. His lips tightened and he came to stand by the fireplace to look down at all of us. "Well? What do you have to say for yourselves?"

Sophie drew in her breath sharply and clutched Christophe's arm. Rafe, predictably, reacted badly to the question. "What do you mean? We're not on trial here."

"Aren't you? Why didn't you report your grandfather's death to the *législateurs* immediately? Why did I have to hear about it from a Homicide detective?"

"Oh," I said softly. "Well, that was a mistake."

"Yes, it was," Nic said. "A bad one. Your grandfather never followed the law or cared much for the *législateurs*. Don't tell me you intend to follow in his footsteps?"

"No, not at all. I-I simply…I forgot I needed to call you first and wait for you to tell us what to do. That's all."

"*Forgot?*"

I flushed and kept on talking. My memory was very hit or miss, especially when I was upset. It was embarrassing and I hated it when someone pointed out things I should have known, but that I'd completely forgotten. "My first instinct was to call the police. I'd never been in a situation like that before. Surely you understand. And it was…distressing."

"*Distressing?* Yes, I imagine finding your grandfather in a pool of blood with…" He turned to the tall man with him, who was leaning negligently against the fireplace mantle and looking supremely bored. "How many stab wounds were there, Taylor?"

"Ten, boss."

"…with ten stab wounds would be a bit distressing… Seems like a crime of passion. Isn't that what the police call it, Taylor?"

"Yeah, they do. Not premeditated. A murder done because of a sudden strong impulse or a sudden rage."

"That's right. Like I said. Like someone who knows a person quite well but has a grudge of some kind against him. A close family member, maybe. Going along from day to day, and then all of a sudden, this person just snaps. You and your grandfather never got along very well, as I recall, Isn't that right, Thibeau?"

Rafe leaped to my defense before I could say a word. "Surely you aren't accusing my brother of killing Abel!"

"I'm not making any accusations. At least not yet. I need to look at the report first and talk to the people in the house that night. I believe we're still waiting for that police report, though, isn't that right, Taylor?"

"That's right, boss."

"And not everyone who lives on the estate is here yet. Taylor, could you go check on the housekeeper and her son?" Taylor nodded and left the room.

"You may as well all get comfortable," Nic said. "I'm not leaving until I get some of my questions answered."

"Listen here…" Rafe began and started to stand up from the chair. He instantly fell back in as if he'd been shoved, yet no one had touched him. There was an almost comical look of surprise on Rafe's face and a second's total silence before I jumped to my feet too. Except I didn't actually jump anywhere, because even though I felt the tension of my muscles, I also felt a force clamping down on me, on my arms and legs and holding me captive in the chair. It was a familiar force—Nic had used it on me often in the past. I strained uselessly, but couldn't budge my own limbs.

I glared up at Nic, who was smirking down at me. He'd pulled that trick on me before in the past when he hadn't wanted to bother with restraints. I'd hated it back then, and I still did. And he knew it.

Taylor walked back in the parlor and shrugged. "The housekeeper and her son both left the grounds."

"Didn't you tell them I wanted to talk to them?"

"I sure did. Guess they left anyway."

"Camille has worked for my grandfather ever since I can remember," I said. "She probably has the same opinion of the *batons* as he did."

Nic's lips tightened as he considered me. "*The housekeeper?* Exactly how much does the fucking housekeeper know about us '*batons*' as you call us? Or witches for that matter?"

"She and her son have lived here for over forty years. She'd have to be pretty stupid not to know about us by now."

Rafe laughed out loud and Nic turned on him. He made a gesture in the air, his big ring flashing in the sunlight streaming in from the windows, and suddenly Rafe's laugh was cut off and my own throat felt tight and constricted. Rafe opened his mouth, but no sound came out.

"Interesting that you find this all so amusing. I will see every person who was in the house that night, is that clear? Do whatever it takes to impress that on your servants."

He had obviously forgotten I couldn't answer him. Apparently, he was using his power against all of us, because I could see my brother's eyes blazing too, and Sophie's face was tight with fear.

"I said, is that clear, Thibeau? Answer me, damn you."

The man he called Taylor nudged his shoulder. "You have him frozen, boss. Might want to let him go if you want an answer."

HEXXED

He scowled at the man and then turned that scowl on me. "Damn
it." He made the gesture again and suddenly the force holding me
was gone.

I coughed and then glared up at him. "It's clear," I said sharply,
glancing over at the rest of my family. They apparently hadn't had
the hold taken off them yet as they were all still frozen, with only
their eyes glowing at me. "Release them. *Please.*"

"Always so polite. Very well. Since you asked me nicely."

Another slight nod and Rafe jumped back up to his feet, his fists
clenched. "You son of a bitch!"

"Rafe! Sit down," I said firmly, and he glanced back at me and
frowned. "Don't underestimate him and don't encourage him to do
even more. That's what he wants."

Nic smiled and winked at him, which made Rafe's face turn an
even brighter red. He threw himself back down in the chair he'd just
vacated, though, only giving Nic a look that promised violence. I
knew Rafe was way outclassed. He was really powerful in his own
right, but Nic was a *baton,* and that put him in a whole different
league.

Nic had never been a cruel or mean person. In fact, he hated
cruelty and had a keen sense of right and wrong. It was what made
him so good at what he did. He was acting this way because of me—
because I'd made him promises in the past that I hadn't kept and I'd
hurt him badly. The fact I hadn't meant to do any of that was
something he didn't know, and something I'd been at pains to hide
from him. No, all this was a little taste of payback for me in his eyes,

and I knew he really wanted to enjoy it. Trouble was, he couldn't quite make himself do it.

"All right," Nic said. "Enough for now. I'm not going to question you further at this time, since the funeral was only a few hours ago, and your sister looks like she's about to pass out. But I'll be back here tomorrow, and I plan to get some answers then. From *all* of you." He looked at each of us in turn and then sauntered past us toward the door, followed by Taylor.

"He's doing it again, damn him!" Rafe said, and I felt the same heaviness in my limbs as before. It wasn't until we heard the door slam behind him that we were finally released. I fell back in my chair and put a hand to my head trying to ease the headache that had hit me about halfway through the conversation.

"Thibeau," Sophie said, sounding frightened. "Why is he treating us like we're some kind of criminals?"

"Because he's an ass, that's why. And he's angry that I didn't call him to report Abel's death, and because I told the police he might be a person of interest."

Sophie's eyes got huge. "You told the police a *baton* killed Grandfather?"

"Not exactly, no. Well, yeah, I guess so, but it was out before I could stop myself. I'll get it straightened out with him tomorrow, honey. Don't worry about it. Christophe, why don't you take Sophie back upstairs so she can rest?"

"Come on, Sophie. Beau's right. You need to lie down," Christophe told her, taking her arm.

26

"I'm okay," she replied, but her voice sounded weak.

"You're as pale as a ghost."

I nodded at Christophe who was escorting her from the room. He looked a little the worse for wear himself, and was quieter than usual as they went up to their room. This had probably been Christophe's first and maybe only experience with *législateurs*. He and Sophie had only been married for about a year. His family's background was in voodoo, which was powerful in its own right, but very different from our kind of magic.

Rafe shoved his hands in his pockets, looking moody. "I was going to go out with some friends, but maybe I shouldn't go now. Maybe *he'll* know and think I should be more grief stricken. *Putain!*"

"Oh, who cares what he thinks? Go ahead and go out. Just don't stay out too late, because like he said, he'll see us bright and early tomorrow."

"Yeah, I'm so scared."

I rubbed my forehead again. "Don't be glib about it, Rafe. The Gaudets aren't our friends. Never have been. And they're dangerous to cross."

"You were pretty friendly with him once upon a time."

"That was a long time ago, and things are different now. Go ahead with your friends and I'll try to get to the bank before they close, though I think it's too late now. I can still make a deposit in the night deposit box I guess. The paperwork will have to wait."

"Okay," he said, moving toward the door. "Be careful. I may not be back 'til late, but I'll see you in the morning."

Fifteen minutes later, I headed out too. I'd been shaken by seeing Nic again and by our tense little confrontation, but it did me no good to dwell on things that couldn't be helped. I dreaded seeing him in the morning, but the sooner my grandfather's death was investigated and the family was cleared, the better it would be for all of us. I had no idea who could have killed him, and maybe the *batons* could shed some light on things. Then maybe we could put some of this behind us and move forward.

Maybe things would be different now. With Abel gone, I was the new head of the family, and as such, I could make some changes. I could ease up on Rafe and let him have the life he wanted, and allow Sophie and Christophe to make their own decisions about their future instead of trying to micromanage it the way my grandfather had done.

I had inherited everything. It was the way it had always been in our family—the oldest child got everything—though it was hardly fair to my younger siblings. I'd share whatever I had with them of course, because it was the right thing to do. I knew that Sophie had wanted to move out for some time now, but Abel had prevented her. Maybe we should even sell this big old mausoleum of a house and split the money, so she'd have a good down payment for a new home. This old place was full of bad memories now, and had been, for me, at least, for a long time.

Abel had threatened more than once to throw me out of this house and cut me off without a cent. He'd been freaked out when he learned how much I liked the BDSM clubs, and had been unpleasantly surprised when I defiantly told him to go ahead and cut me off, because I didn't give a fuck what he thought. It had been another nail in my coffin when I taunted him, saying I not only liked to be manhandled, tied up and fucked, but that I preferred men to be the ones to do it. I came to regret throwing that in his face.

I was pretty sure he had known Rafe liked men too, but he'd never mentioned it, bringing the brunt of his wrath down on me, his heir, instead. He'd called me sick, perverted and unnatural and had used it and the fact that I was gay against me pretty effectively. In fact, he'd come close to destroying me.

Since both Rafe and I were gay, only Sophie and her husband Christophe were left to carry on the family blood line—at least in my grandfather's mind. Their children, however, would be Decoudreaus, and not Delessards, a fact that had not escaped old Abel, and in fact, had filled him with fury. He had demanded that I marry and give him an heir, and he had spent the better part of the last year searching for a suitable candidate to be my wife. Suitable, in my grandfather's eyes, meant rich and easy to control.

I was perfectly willing to bring children into the world through a surrogate, and I had always wanted a family. But I had steadfastly refused to find some poor, unsuspecting woman and ruin her life by marrying her, when the most I could ever offer her would be friendship. Abel, however, refused to accept no for an answer and wanted me in a "proper" relationship. He had made elaborate threats if I continued to refuse, and I had almost run out of excuses. In fact, on the day before he was murdered, we'd had a loud, epic fight in the dining room at dinner, with Abel yelling that he would cut me out of his will and make Rafe the heir instead. When I told him to go ahead, he'd flown into an even greater rage. Thank God all that was over now.

It was uncharacteristically quiet in the house as I made my way out to my car. As I went out, I could see Camille and Emmanuel's car was, indeed, still not parked in front of their cottage. Camille had come over to the house early that morning, so before I had gone upstairs, I'd given her the rest of the day off. At her age, she must have been exhausted, but she had certainly cleared out fast when Nic had shown up. I didn't make anything of that—she believed the way my grandfather had, and didn't recognize the *batons* as having any authority over her. They didn't, as a matter of fact, since she didn't have any magic. That didn't mean they couldn't make things difficult for her and her son, though. I'd have a talk with her in the morning.

The black wreath hung accusingly on the door as I closed it softly behind me, reminding me this was supposed to be a house of mourning, and I should probably wait until tomorrow to conduct business of any kind. But I wasn't that much of a hypocrite. I wasn't sorry Abel was dead—though I had been appalled by the manner of his death. I wouldn't pretend to be grief stricken just for appearances' sake. Abel had cost me everything once upon a time, and I had never forgiven him for it, no matter how hard I'd tried. Seeing Nic again had been a bitter reminder of what I'd lost.

Even the skies seemed to agree with my foul, bitter mood, because as I came down the steps, an ominous rumble came from the dark clouds overhead and a cold rain began pelting down. I pulled my jacket up to help cover my head and ran for the car. But as I reached for the door handle, I heard a rush come from behind me and something crashed into the back of my head. Stunned, I sagged to my knees on the soggy ground, and heard a deep growl above me as the second blow fell. That blow made me crash head first into the side of my car and everything went black.

Chapter Two

Struggling slowly back up to consciousness, I became aware almost immediately of two things—I was naked and lying on my side with both my hands and feet tightly bound with some kind of heavy chains, and I was freezing. My head pounded. I was so dizzy that for one frantic moment I thought I might throw up. Since most of my face was covered with what felt like a stiff and unyielding leather mask, that would have been beyond horrible. I was able to breathe through my nose and keep it down—barely—but my mouth was stuffed and stretched by what felt like a ball gag, judging by the tight band around the back of my head and the taste of rubber in my mouth. If I did throw up, I'd surely choke to death. There weren't any eyeholes in the mask so I couldn't see anything.

I tried moving my bare feet around to see if I could touch anything and almost immediately touched something cold and hard, like metal. Then an engine started and I felt the vibrations of movement, realizing then that someone must have thrown me in the trunk of a car, maybe even my own vehicle. There was nothing I could do but endure it as the car moved swiftly, taking turns way too fast as if the driver was panicked and trying to make a quick getaway.

I realized too, with despair, that no one at my home would even think to look for me for many hours yet—probably not until morning. If I was being hauled away somewhere to be murdered like my grandfather, there wasn't much I was going to be able to do to stop it. I'd still try, of course. I had been calling on my magic ever since I swam back up into consciousness, but it was still stubbornly nonexistent. Someone must not have known that, though, because with my mouth stuffed with a gag, they had made sure I wouldn't be able to speak a spell. With the tight chains on my wrists and feet that were probably iron, my magic, had it still existed, would have been bound anyway.

The car continued to take turns that were way too fast and despite the small space I'd been confined in, I was being bounced and tossed around quite a bit. I thought I could hear the sounds of traffic around me too, which was comforting in some ways. At least I wasn't being taken out to some lonely dirt road to be shot, my body abandoned and left to rot in a ditch.

After an interminable time, the car came to an abrupt halt and I expected the trunk to open any second. But nothing happened. I had another moment of panic when I wondered if my kidnapper was just going to leave me here, trussed up and helpless, to die of slow asphyxiation when all the air was finally gone from the trunk. It was already getting harder and harder to breathe. But no, I hadn't heard any car door slamming, so the kidnapper was still inside the car. A voice came from outside the vehicle then, seeming close by, but it didn't sound like anyone I knew.

"What's up, man? Why did you want me to meet you out here in the back of the club?"

A low murmuring answered him, and I knew the person inside the car was purposely keeping his voice low so I wouldn't recognize it. The other voice came again.

"What? This is some bullshit, dude. I could lose my job if the owner finds out. What's this about anyway? I thought you wanted to get geared up with some crank."

More murmuring. Then, "Kidnapping fantasy? What the fuck? Are you fucking *crazy*?"

The car door slammed and I heard the footsteps coming around to the back of the car. I heard the trunk lid lift and felt a cold breeze on my naked skin. I heard a quick intake of breath. "What the fuck?" the voice said again, sounding very young. "Is he okay?"

I moaned and tried to lunge out of the back, but strong arms caught me around the waist and held me in place. "He's fine," said a harsh, raspy voice. "He likes it. Just help me get him out."

A few seconds passed and then I was taken out of the back of the car and stood swaying for a moment on my feet. Rough hands fastened what must have been another iron chain around my neck. My ankles were freed and I was dragged roughly forward. A voice sounded right in my ear. "I'm taking you inside. Cooperate or I'll kill you right here."

Whoever it was jerked the chain so hard it almost pulled me off my feet. I could hear the other voice saying something softly, maybe protesting the rough treatment, but the kidnapper laughed. "He likes

it, I told you," he ground out. "Come on, asshole, move!" He pushed
my back, again almost knocking me off my feet, but I somehow
managed to get them under me and stumble forward. I had no idea
what was happening, but we were moving toward the sound of
people talking and that had to be a good thing. I knew this person
with the rough voice wanted to harm me, but if we were around
other people, then surely someone would object to this. Someone
would help me. They had to!

Suddenly, I was violently thrown up against a cold wall, and I felt
the sharp prick of a needle in my arm. "Time to fly," the voice
whispered in my ear and almost immediately I felt the drug he had
shot into me racing through my veins.

I heard loud music thumping ahead of me as I was dragged or
alternately pushed along. I could also hear increasingly loud moans
and groans and the sounds of leather striking flesh. With a sick,
sinking feeling, I knew where this kidnapper must have taken me—it
was one of the clubs that specialized in BDSM and maybe even one
of the ones I used to frequent. And not just any BDSM. In New
Orleans there were a few clubs in the seediest, darkest fringes of the
Quarter that catered to the worst of the sadists and masochists, the
ones other BDSM clubs had banned because safe, sane and
consensual weren't words in their vocabulary. They were the ones
whose members wanted to play in a dungeon where literally
anything was allowed to happen, and often did.

The smells of men's cologne, liquor and stale sweat were
unmistakable to someone who had spent a good deal of time in a

club like this one, the way I had at one time in my life. Some of the clubs in this part of the city were so extreme that a naked man, obviously drugged and being led around in a mask and chains wouldn't make anyone think twice. Some of the clubs even had rumors swirling around them about the occasional dead body being found in the shallow, brackish water of Lake Pontchartrain, with ligatures on the wrists and ankles and evidence of whips and cane marks, burns and cuts all over it. Some even had all the blood drained from their bodies. But those were only rumors…or so everyone said.

Even if this wasn't that kind of club, I could tell I was already in the back part of it where the dungeons were. This man had apparently bypassed the main entrance where someone in management might possibly have stopped or questioned this. We had obviously been let in a back entrance.

He unchained my arms, but I was becoming dazed and almost unconscious from the drug. I was alternately hot and then cold and could barely breathe. The kidnapper had to support my weight. He spread my arms and legs apart to strap me to a hard, unyielding surface by iron chains again. Possibly a St. Andrew's Cross. A hard hand grabbed the back of my neck and viciously squeezed as the voice sounded in my ear again.

"Stay still," he said and whacked his hand against the wound on the back of my head. My head was already throbbing from whatever he'd hit me with, so I couldn't stop the deep groan that came out of my throat as my knees buckled.

HEXXED

"You like this, mother-fucker? You like being punished? Let's see just how much punishment you can take." He hit me then with his fist, a hard, savage blow to my nose. Blood spurted from it immediately, dripping down onto my obscenely stretched lips, the blood clogging my nostrils and making it nearly impossible to breathe. He wasn't through with me yet, though, because next he slammed his fist into my eye.

He stepped away, but the searing pain of a thick cane exploded across my back. I tried to scream, but I was choking on the blood and the gag and I couldn't make much of a sound. I was afraid there wasn't anyone around to hear me anyway, except for the man torturing me, and I wasn't sure if I'd die first from the beating or from suffocation or from choking to death on my own blood. I tipped my head down and endured, my chest heaving to draw in air. Another blow fell and then another. So many and with so much force, I lost count. It had been a long time since I used to play hard and even then I'd never taken this kind of beating. He was killing me, slowly and methodically and there was nothing I could do about it. My knees buckled, and I sagged helplessly, hopelessly against the chains that bound me.

It had only been minutes since he'd started, but I I wasn't sure how much longer I could last. Blows rained down on my back, my hips and my thighs, even my balls and one or two on the back of my head. It was obvious by now that the sonofabitch was going to kill me. Blow after blow, layered one on top of another, and I could feel the skin on my body breaking open like too ripe fruit. Blood was

37

trickling down my back and my legs and puddling by my feet. I began to lose consciousness, drifting away on the knife edge of pain. The blackness over my eyes formed itself into sparks that swarmed in front of my eyes and I started fading out. Just then, I heard another voice, this one sounding farther away, but coming closer and getting louder. As loud as Gabriel's trumpet. That was fitting, actually, as I was pretty sure I was minutes away from dying.

"Putain de bordel de merde! Give me that goddamn cane! You're killing him!"

I heard the sounds of a scuffle, and some loud cursing, then someone running away. Almost immediately, strong arms came around my waist to support me as the chains were take off my wrists and I was lowered to the floor. Next came my ankles and then I was free, but my entire body throbbed with pain and I felt my consciousness slipping away. The mask was eased off and the hateful gag pried out of my mouth. I was picked up and carried over to some soft surface, and whoever saved me placed me carefully on top of it. My back was so painful, though, I cried out in agony, and my savior quickly pulled me back up to a sitting position. That was agonizing too, but easier to get air. I drew in a long, shuddery breath of it, and he started to wipe away the blood that was still clogging my nose and mouth.

That's when I heard a loud gasp.

"Thibeau! Beau! My God, what the fuck happened here?"

XXXX

38

HEXXED

Nic

Taylor and I had left the old Delessard mansion that afternoon in the rain, the weather still matching my mood perfectly. I told Taylor to stop outside the gate, trying to decide if I should go back inside. I wasn't finished with Thibeau, yet, and I'd known that the second I'd walked through the doors back to the car.

I'd also acted like an ass and a bully, and I hadn't seemed to be able to help myself. A big part of me wanted to go back in there and make it up to him. Seeing him again had hurt a lot worse than I'd expected it to, because, God, he hadn't changed much in the last two years. He'd lost a little weight, maybe, and he was a bit pale. His hair might have been shorter than it had been the last time I'd seen him, but he was still far too beautiful for his own good. And for mine. When I left the house just then, I felt like I'd left a part of myself behind, and I hated it. I hated him!

I wanted to take him in my arms and never let him go.

The fence that went around the property was hedged by overgrown shrubbery, and Taylor parked the car behind the nearest of the large old oak trees that lined the road leading up to the house, while I contemplated what to do next.

Taylor was a good driver—maybe even a great one, but his particular skill set lay in a different direction. He was ex Special Forces and all muscle, and had been with me for over ten years. He traveled with me wherever I went as both a driver and a bodyguard, though I had little need of the latter. Still, he was handy to have around, did as he was told and never questioned me or balked at anything I asked him to do. He was also my best friend, and knew all my secrets, as I knew his. He knew where all the bodies were buried. Figuratively speaking, of course.

I sat there for a few minutes, just brooding as I gazed at Ravenwood. The old place hadn't changed since I'd last seen it, except perhaps to grow even shabbier and more run down. The words, "how the mighty have fallen," repeated themselves over and over in my head. They could have been written about this very house and family.

From a distance, and if you squinted your eyes a bit, it was still a lovely old mansion. Built probably a hundred years before, it had the look of old New Orleans with its double-gallery style. It was a two-story house with a side-gabled roof, set well back from the large, ornate gate. Its two-story gallery that wrapped around each side sagged a little now, its lacy ironwork rusty in places. The columns supporting the upper gallery looked a little shaky, and the whole structure could have used a generous slap of paint.

A couple of cars had left the grounds since we came back through the gates, one of them driven by Rafe, Thibeau's defiant younger brother. Good. I preferred not to have an audience for the more personal things I wanted to say to Beau when I went back inside. I figured his sister and her husband had gone up to their room by now, since she'd looked like she was about to faint when I was there. I was sorry if I'd upset her, but she was, unfortunately, collateral damage. Beau had been the one I was after.

I was gearing myself up to go back in when an old Ford Taurus like the one Thibeau drove came tearing through the gates. A man was driving, but I couldn't tell if it was Thibeau, because by this time the rain was pouring down, and the driver kept his face turned away so I got only a flash of it. The back windows were tinted so dark it was impossible to see inside or to see if there was anyone in the back seat.

I had felt a tingle of something, though—just the slightest prickle of awareness and uneasiness as the car passed by, and I knew then that it had been Thibeau in that car. I had felt him, a prickly awareness that I knew in my soul.

"Follow that car, Taylor. That was Thibeau."

"Okay, boss." He called me "boss" just to annoy me. He put the car in gear but we were facing the wrong direction, so we lost a little time turning the car around in the narrow road.

The Taurus had already pulled way ahead of us, and when it reached the highway, it must have really taken off because it was completely out of sight. Taylor managed to close in on it some, but I could find him again when I needed to, even if I had to use a little magic to do it, and I didn't want Thibeau to figure out he was being followed. I was curious about where he was going and who he might be going to meet. As we got closer to town, Friday traffic set in, along with the bad weather, and only Taylor's skills kept us from getting hopelessly snarled up in traffic.

When we got stopped for yet another traffic jam I'd finally had enough. I was antsy, and feeling stymied in my attempt to make Thibeau answer for siccing the police on me. I had the righteous anger of the unjustly accused going for me, and I had been more than ready to confront him again, this time face to face and alone, without his family around as a buffer. I had planned to make him admit he was wrong. I needed to hear him say he was sorry for everything he'd done to me between now and the last time I'd seen him two years ago. I needed him on his knees for me, looking up at me with those big, beautiful dark eyes of his and begging my forgiveness. And that thought gave me an erection that had me squirming in my seat and adjusting myself.

I suppose the things I wanted to do to him were unrealistic and unreasonable, but I'd never been exactly prudent when it came to Thibeau Delessard. Not since the first time I'd met him in the club in the worst section of Faubourg Tremé, a neighborhood best avoided by tourists at night, with parts of it considered unsafe by respectable people. The club didn't really have an official name—or if it did, I'd never heard it.

Most people just called it LaRue's after the drag queen who used to own the place, though she had gone on to her reward in the late 1980s. It was hardcore—a rough and shady BDSM club, only for serious players or thugs who pretended to be Doms. Even the fucking subs in that place were scary.

I had dropped in a time or two, when I was younger and wilder and in the mood for trouble, and that club was normally a place I

could find a lot of it. It seemed like a lifetime ago, and I'd made
Thibeau stop going to it after we met. Even considering how
powerful his magic was, I didn't want him anywhere near the place.
It would have been too easy to slip a drug into his drink or a
hypodermic needle in his arm. Besides, he was mine and I was a
possessive bastard.

"Damn it, he's going to LaRue's, Taylor," I said, realizing what
neighborhood we were near. I felt restless and scared at the idea of
Beau in LaRue's in a vulnerable state of mind. Of course, he would
go there, because I had once strictly forbidden it. But hell, it was
only early evening, on the same day as his grandfather's funeral. I
had to admit I was a little shocked.

I'd been surprised when I saw the crowd at the house as we
arrived, but we'd figured out pretty soon that it must be the funeral
or the wake after, and Taylor had reminded me the police don't
release the body for a while after a murder. It had been just over a
week since Abel had been killed, so that was about right, I supposed.
They'd had to wait for the autopsy to be done.

Taylor gave me a look in the rear view before he nodded and
headed toward La Rue's. I didn't pay him to give me advice, and he
wisely refrained from doing so. I was feeling reckless, angry and
wound up—I wasn't sure what I would do if I went inside that club
and found Thibeau there—especially if I found him with another
man. I'd really counted on being able to see Thibeau again at his
house and make him pay for running his mouth to the police. Hell,
let's face it, I'd just really counted on seeing him again. Full stop.

But if I found him at the BDSM club where we'd first met, and if he was naked or nearly so and wearing another man's marks on his skin, I couldn't be responsible for what I might do to him.

Every time I thought of Thibeau Delessard, and it was way more often than I liked to admit, I thought of that line from that fucking heartbreaking movie that straight people liked to make fun of and gay people found to be uncomfortable, because it had a little too much truth in it, even today. The line that had become so iconic that it had become a joke—though nothing about it was funny in the least. "I wish I knew how to quit you." That line pretty much summed up how I felt about Thibeau. I'd never stopped loving him. And at the same time hating him for ruining my life. I couldn't seem to move on from him and that infuriated me most of all.

My mood was growing even murkier, just like the streets in this really bad neighborhood we were headed for, and a part of me relished what kind of trouble I might be able to get into. We passed drug dealers lounging on the corners and a variety of closed and shuttered store fronts. Fifteen minutes later, Taylor pulled up to the front of the club and I got out. I looked around for Thibeau's car, but he must have parked around the back. "Wait for me," I told him, "and you'd better stay with the car in this neighborhood."

"Planned to," he replied calmly as ever, and I smiled, pitying the fool who saw the expensive car and thought the man driving it might be an easy mark. Taylor was all muscle. That and the Beretta he was always packing in the holster under his arm would be all the protection he needed.

HEXXED

I went inside the dingy lobby. Respectable clubs had rules posted in the front, with someone checking people in at the door to make sure subs were able to articulate their limits and not so drugged up they didn't know they were still in the world. This place had none of that, as it was a far cry from respectable. I paid the ten-dollar cover charge and stepped through the torn black curtains to go into the drinking area, wrinkling my nose at the stale smell of booze, vomit and cum. Hooks and chains dangled from the ceiling in places and various benches and sawhorses were set up around the corners of the room. Good to see that nothing much ever changed.

At this time of day, I hadn't expected to see anybody here, but there were already a few Doms sitting in the main bar at the tables with subs at their feet or hanging off them, and two female subs at the bar, wearing very little. One was only wearing a harness. She was a curvy, bleached blonde, and she slipped off one of the stools and started lurching drunkenly toward me. I sent her a look that made her back off. I didn't want a sub tonight—at least not anybody except Thibeau. I wondered if Thibeau was in the back with some other guy. I might just fuck somebody up if they got in my way right now, and nobody needed that. Least of all me.

The only man I was interested in had been hiding from me behind his wards, amulets, and restraining orders for the past two years. I headed down the back hallway, looking into the open doors as I passed. A sub was being double penetrated in one room and some boys were getting spanked with a thin chain flogger in another. Some electric play and even some knife play caught my attention

45

only long enough for me to make sure none of the subs involved were Thibeau.

Just when I was beginning to think I was wrong about Beau coming to La Rue's, and we'd have to search the other clubs in the area, I heard heavy breathing and muffled moans and cries coming from the last room on the hall, along with the thud of a thick cane getting up close and personal with naked flesh. I went to the door and thought for a moment I had been somehow transported to the bedroom of the Marquis de Sade. blood puddled around the feet of the poor guy hanging from the St. Andrews Cross, and his back, ass and legs were a mass of bloody welts. As I stood there in shock, the so-called Dom wielding the thick cane landed a blow right on the back of the sub's head and my own head almost exploded. The beating—and that's what this was—had been only going on for a few minutes with a cane as big around as my thumb, but a lot of damage had already been inflicted. I thought that last blow might have killed the poor guy because he never even flinched when it landed. Then I heard a low moan.

"What the fuck?" I yelled as the sonofabitch pulled back his arm and landed another fucking hard blow right across the sub's kidneys, making me wince in sympathy. I tore the cane from his hand, and he whirled in surprise to look at me. He was wearing a black mask that showed nothing but his startled brown eyes and full lips.

"Putain de bordel de merde! Give me that goddamn cane! You're killing him!"

The so-called Dom beating the sub hesitated for only a second, staring at me, his eyes round with shock, then threw his bloody cane at my face and bolted from the room. I hurled a spell after him, but I was rattled so my aim was off. It ricocheted off the wall by his head with a crackling sound. He ducked and kept running out of the room and toward the back door that was usually kept locked. I would have gone after him, but I knew I had to render immediate aid to the poor bastard on the St. Andrews cross.

I hurried over to the man and took him down as carefully as I could, lowering him first to his knees. He was gasping by this time so I eased off the mask and took out the huge ball gag in his mouth, so he could take a breath. His face was a mass of blood from what might have been a broken nose. I put an arm around his waist and supported him over to a bed in the corner, letting him first lie down and then sit up when that hurt too much. At least as best he could. I could really see then how badly he was hurt. I pulled off the none too clean sheet on the bed to wipe off some of his face, so he could breathe a little better and only then did I get a good look at him. And I almost lost it.

"Thibeau! Beau! My God, what the fuck has happened here?"

He peered up at me through his one good eye, and I saw his pupil was like a pinpoint. He'd been drugged and recently. He tried to speak through swollen, bloody lips. "N-Nic?" he gasped out, his voice incredulous and cracking. He collapsed against me sobbing, and I held him as gently as I could, hardly daring to touch his poor back. My fingers skimmed over it, feeling the welts the cane had placed there. I instinctively began whispering the words of a healing spell, and some of the deeper wounds began to stitch back together. I spoke another one to ease his pain.

"Oh, *minou*," I said softly in his ear, and it was what I used to call him. He'd hated it then, but it was as if all the years of bitterness between us just dissolved into thin air when I saw how hurt he was. He needed me, and that was all I needed to know. "Beau, what happened to you? Who the fuck was that guy?"

He shook his head, gasping, and I quickly fished my cell phone out of my pocket and called Taylor. "Get in here fast. Back room, last door on the left. Hurry! I think you better call an ambulance too."

"N-no! No ambulance!" Thibeau cried and tried to grab my phone.

"Thibeau," I said, pulling my hand up and angling my head back to look down into his poor, battered face. "I've got to get you out of here and take you to a hospital."

"No! No h-hospital!" he gasped, pulling away. "Please, Nic, *please!* P-promise me! No hospital!"

"You're badly hurt, *cher*. You need to go to the ER."

"No!" he cried, and tried to get up off the bed, stumbling and almost falling to his knees. I caught him around the waist before he fell, but winced as my hand touched a deep, bloody welt across his lower back. I settled him back onto the bed, trying to gentle him, like I would a wild animal.

"Okay, okay, no worries. No hospital, *minou*. Whatever you say. I'll just take you home, okay?"

The door burst open and Taylor charged inside, his hand under his jacket, and I knew he was gripping his Beretta. "Boss, what's going on?" he said, a little out of breath and then stopped short as he caught sight of Thibeau. He looked from Thibeau to me and his face drained of color. "*Boss…*"

"No, whatever you're thinking—just—*no*! I never touched him. I found some asshole beating him, and just got him down off the equipment, but he's badly hurt. He says he doesn't want a hospital, but we need to get him out of this fucking place now!"

He nodded and stepped past me to the bed, stripping off the dingy, stained sheet while I held Thibeau upright, still supporting him with my arm around his waist. Taylor wrapped the sheet around him and I picked Beau up in my arms, and strode past him for the exit. Taylor was right behind me.

The people in the front room barely glanced up as we passed, but that was the kind of place this was. Had Thibeau gone back to clubs like this again? What the hell had he been thinking? How had so much damage been done to him so fast? At most, because of the traffic jam, I had only been at most thirty minutes or so behind him. The so-called Dom had inflicted a massive amount of damage in that time.

I put Beau down in the back seat, and got in beside him, holding tightly to his hand. He was shaking with reaction and shock, so

Taylor put the heat on full blast, and I stripped off my jacket to put over him.

"I wish you'd let us take you a hospital," I said softly, but he immediately jerked away and started shaking his head.

"*Nooo*, please! *No, Nic*! No hospital! Just-just d-drop me off somewhere. I can get my b-brother to pick me up."

"You're kidding, right? If you think I'm leaving you like this, you're crazy." He flinched at the word and drew up in a ball in the corner of the back seat by the window, and I cursed myself for scaring him. I wanted to hold him, but I didn't want to upset him anymore, so I began muttering calming spells over him and gradually he eased enough for his body to slump over. I thought for one awful moment that he'd lost consciousness and panicked a little, but his breathing was even and calmer, and the more I chanted, the more his body relaxed. I gently pulled him over to me. He was unresisting, his muscles having lost that desperate tension. I settled him so his head rested on my knees, then pulled back the dirty sheet and my fingers skimmed over his back, as I began working on healing the mass of welts there.

The air grew thick with incantations as I worked, until Taylor finally said, "Boss, ease up a little, will you? You're putting me to sleep up here and I think you're fogging the windshield."

I huffed out a half-laugh and "eased up" as Taylor had suggested. I had repaired a lot of the damage to Beau's flesh, but I was afraid his emotional damage was going to be much worse. I was anxious to know how he'd gotten himself in this situation, but now, when he was only about half-conscious, wasn't the time to pressure him for details. First, I had to get him home, cleaned up and put to bed. Talking could come later if he felt like it. He shifted restlessly on my lap and partially sat up, still leaning heavily against me and wincing only a little, so I knew my efforts had paid off a bit. He sighed like a tired child and put his head on my shoulder.

"Am I dreaming? Nic, tell me. Are you really here?"

"I'm here, *cher*. I'm taking you home."

I couldn't help stroking his cheek and tracing over his lips with my finger. He was so beautiful, even like this—I'd almost forgotten how much. I never thought I'd have the chance to touch him again, so I took advantage of the moment and I wasn't sorry for it. I looked up and met Taylor's gaze in the rear-view mirror and shook my head. "Goddammit," I said.

He nodded sadly. "I know, boss. Guess it's too late now to tell you to be careful."

I looked back down at the long eyelashes sweeping over Thibeau's cheek and nodded. "Afraid so," I said. Who the hell was I fooling? It had been too late the second I saw him again. I kept on stroking his soft hair all the way back to Ravenwood.

Chapter Three

When we got to the gate outside Ravenwood, I nudged Thibeau awake. "Is the gate locked?"

He shook his head, still looking groggy as Taylor pulled up and stopped long enough to get out and swing the gates wide open. We slowly pulled up the driveway toward the dark house. Not a single light had been left on, not even the front porch. I got out first, looking up at the front of the house. I thought I saw the twitch of a curtain upstairs, but when I looked again, I didn't see any sign of life at all. Wrapping an arm around Thibeau's waist, I helped him up the stairs to the wide, wrap-around porch and up to the front door. The door was open, and I saw Thibeau notice and frown in confusion. I was immediately hit by a feeling of dread as I stepped inside. It was almost a feeling of foreboding and I was uncomfortable in the extreme. I recognized the feel of dark magic right away.

There was a warlock in the house.

"Somebody here wants you dead, Thibeau," I said softly and looked around the dark entry for the threat, which felt immediate and palpable. It was a new threat too. It hadn't been there when Taylor and I were at that house earlier. The air was stuffy and hard to breathe and felt greasy on my skin. All classic signs of a warlock operating close by. "Be vigilant. Shoot anybody that comes out of the dark at us. He's got a warlock after him," I said over my shoulder to Taylor, and he nodded, instinctively pulling out his gun again.

The house itself—the very ether—felt cold and dark and stripped of power, and it shouldn't have. Not with a powerful witch like Abel having lived there for so many years. Not to mention Thibeau and his younger brother and sister, all of them witches. But...*were* they? I glanced down at Thibeau and realized I felt nothing coming from him. Caught up in the drama of seeing him again, I hadn't paid attention to it earlier but he was practically a void, with hardly any power at all.

Which was impossible—from the first time I'd met Thibeau well over two years ago, I had known right away he was a practitioner. His powers had been strong back then, practically radiating off him and lighting him up with inner fire. And since there was only one other family in town that had that kind of high magic, I'd known immediately at the time that he had to be a Delessard. Of course, that opened up a whole new field of difficulty, but what on earth could have happened to strip him like this?

"We have to get him to his bedroom," I said to Taylor, feeling even more protective of Thibeau than ever, and Taylor nodded, his gaze scanning all the dark corners of the entry way.

"Is there anyone else at home?" he asked, and Thibeau surprised me by softly answering. He'd been so quiet for so long that I'd thought he was barely conscious. He sounded weak, but perfectly coherent.

"My sister and her husband are in their part of the house. My brother's gone out. He probably won't be home 'til morning."

"Where's your bedroom?"

"Top of the stairs, second door on the right."

He started toward the stairs, but I put my arm around his waist to support him. He looked up at me in surprise and blushed, a sweet pink stain spreading over his cheeks, but he didn't protest. I got him to his room, with Taylor right behind us, and took him straight to the bathroom I could see through the open door. He was practically covered in blood, and I needed to get him cleaned up some so I could better assess the damage. Taylor stayed outside in the bedroom, settling himself in a chair by Thibeau's bed and quietly watching the door.

I sat Thibeau down on the toilet seat so I could adjust the water in the shower. When I had it fixed—and it took a couple of minutes for the water to warm up—I stripped him of the dirty sheet and threw it in a corner. He blushed again and turned his head away, but I ignored him and helped him step inside the shower. His body was as beautiful as it had always been, and it wasn't like I hadn't seen him before. In fact, I'd probably traced over every inch of his skin with my tongue at one time or another. I gave him his privacy and left him alone as the warm water washed over him, only checking to make sure the welts on his back were mostly closed and not starting to bleed again.

Healing up cuts and welts, even as severe as the ones on Thibeau's body, was a simple kind of magic. On the level of folk magic, really, and could be done by any reasonably skilled practitioner. Maybe not as quickly as I'd done it for Thibeau, but still, it was easy, and one of the first things a witch learned how to do. A lot of people here in New Orleans practiced voodoo. Mine was a different kind of magic, we considered it to be high magic, and for me, it was as easy as tapping into the etheric flow. Or I should say, normally it would have been. But this house didn't seem to have any energy flow to speak of. It had been ruthlessly stripped and not long ago.

The problem was that I didn't have any way to restore my energy without tapping into the ether, and I'd used up a lot of mine in healing Thibeau. Another problem was that I'd felt a concentrated negative energy, all of it rushing toward us as we came in the house. I had it stopped for now, but I needed to get him out of there and fast before there was another attack of some kind. I stepped out the bathroom door and went over to his dresser, looking for something soft for him to wear. Taylor watched me steadily, keeping one eye on the door to the outside hallway. He could feel it too.

Taylor was what was known as a *léger*. That literally translated to "lightweight" and it referred to his latent powers, and certainly not his personality or his body. It meant that he wasn't exactly a witch, but he had some latent magic in his bones and blood. It more than likely accounted for the fact that he was still alive after all the times he'd been wounded in Afghanistan and elsewhere. What most people called "luck" was nine times out of ten a little bit of *léger* magic. Probably ten percent of the population had it passed down to them from some distant ancestor who had been a seriously talented practitioner.

I'd known Taylor had it within the first five minutes of meeting him all those years ago when he interviewed for the position as my driver. Of course, over the years, I'd come to rely on him in more ways than I could count, including that sixth sense of his, and he was a member of the *législateurs,* though he disliked using magic and only did it when I insisted. Even then he had to use a wand, which helped him focus and direct his power.

"Be ready to get out of here as soon as I get him dressed. It's not safe for him to be here."

"What's wrong with this place, boss?"

"You feel it too? I thought you probably could—it's so strong. Someone has been stripping it for more power."

"What do you mean?"

"This family has lived here a long time and they're powerful witches. All that is imprinted on the atmosphere—on the ether itself. And somebody has been tapping into it so much it's stripping it of all its power. It has to be a warlock. Either someone in the family or someone who comes here often. But it's recent, I think. Since we left here this afternoon. Look around for hexes. Maybe near his bed."

"Hexes? *Here in my room?* No way." Thibeau said, stepping out of the bathroom wrapped in a big towel. He was shivering still, from the cold in this house and no doubt from shock. I tossed him the flannel shirt I'd found and he wrapped it around his shoulders.

"You need to get warm." I went over to him and pushed a pair of gray sweats into his hand too and some warm socks. "Put that shirt on and get these on too. Tell me who it was in LaRue's that did this to you, Beau."

"I don't know who it was."

I made an impatient sound and he touched my arm. "Nic, I'm telling you the truth. I left the house soon after you were here. I was going to the bank to make a late deposit. Someone must have been waiting for me by my car. They hit me on the back of the head and I woke up in the trunk of my car."

"And you really have no idea who it could have been?"

"No, I swear it."

"All right. We'll talk about it later, but right now we need to go."

"Go? Go where? I just got home."

"You can't stay here, Thibeau. Someone here wants you dead."

His eyes widened and he looked at me like I was crazy. "No, that's impossible. Only my family is here and none of them would ever harm me."

"Nevertheless."

"Look at this, boss."

I turned to see Taylor holding up a small dish. "I found this shoved under his bed."

Rich, black dirt lay in the shape of an X across the plate. On top of that a photo of Thibeau that looked like it had been cut from his driver's license. Someone had taken a hole-puncher to his eyes in the picture and then drew vertical lines over the mouth with a magic marker to make it appear as if his mouth had been sewn shut. A small piece of folded paper lay on top—I knew that if I unfolded it, I'd find Thibeau's name written on it. The folded little package had one quarter turned down and the word *Crossed* written on it in a childish hand.

"It's a hex. A crossing spell for an enemy," I said, looking over at Thibeau. "It's voodoo, and this dirt is from a crossroad or a graveyard. Maybe a mixture of both."

"And you think that's for me?" Thibeau asked incredulously. "No fucking way."

"How do you explain it then?"

"I don't," he replied, his face turning red. He looked at me suspiciously. "How do I know you didn't bring it with you?"

I just stared at him. I was frightening him, and he'd had a rough night, so I made allowances and I wasn't going to get into it with him, especially not there in that house. We had things to talk about, no doubt about that. And I planned to—just not here.

"I'm sorry," he said, after a moment of us just staring at each other. "I...I appreciate everything you've done for me. Of course, I do. But-but this is too crazy...this is... He cleared his throat and tried to cough. "This is... *Shit!*" he started to cough again, and his eyes got wide. He stopped talking and tried to swallow and then clear his throat again forcefully. He made a harsh noise in his throat and started gagging. He looked up at me, his eyes panicked and staring. "C-can't bre...c-can't ..." he managed to say around lips that were rapidly swelling. I pulled him close to me and he opened

58

his mouth, displaying a tongue that was swelling right before my eyes and turning dark purple.

"N-Ni…!" he tried to say my name around his distorted tongue, his eyes rolling back in his head in sheer panic.

"Try to breathe through your nose!" I yelled at him and pushed more magic at him. His face was rapidly turning blue and his eyes were bulging.

"Goddammit!" I turned to Taylor. "Give me your pen!"

Taylor looked shocked too and totally baffled for a second, but fumbled for his ballpoint pen and shoved it at me with trembling hands.

"Open it and take out the refill! *Hurry*, damn it! My magic's not working!"

I pushed Thibeau to his knees and felt for the opening in the membrane below his Adam's apple before the firmer cartilage of his trachea began. He was clawing at me, in a desperate panic, because his airway was completely closed off now by his bulging tongue and horribly swollen lips. I had found the opening, so I managed to look him in the eye for a fleeting second.

"Hold on, Thibeau! Don't be scared, *cher*. I'm going to help!"

Taylor passed me the pen and I held tightly to Beau, pulled my arm back and jabbed downward with the hollow point of the pen directly into his throat. The pen would act as a tube to keep the opening clear until a more secure airway could be maintained, or until I could get him the fuck out of this house. It was a ludicrous kind of tracheotomy, and I was a little shocked it actually worked.

But it was the best I could come up with on short notice and I thanked all the TV I watched as a kid for giving me the idea. This place was too drained of power for my magic to do much good, and besides, I didn't want to strip myself completely before we got the hell out of there.

Taylor caught Thibeau's hands and held them down as he tried to scream and clutch at the tube sticking out of his throat, but gradually, as we held onto him, he realized he wasn't suffocating any more and though he was still freaking the fuck out, he managed to be more still and let us help him. Blood was trickling down his neck and staining his chest again, but that was the least of my worries.

I swept him up in my arms for the second time that night and started for the door. My eyes met Taylor's and he held his Beretta ready, clearly intending to shoot anyone or anything we might encounter on the way out of this mausoleum and sort it all out later on. "*Allons!* Bring that hex with us. And Taylor…"

"Yes, boss?"

"Shoot to kill," I said.

"No other way to do it, boss."

As it turned out, we didn't see a soul anywhere in the house as we came rushing down the stairs and got out to my car. Immediately outside the old house, I could breathe more easily, and I hoped it was affecting Thibeau the same way. This time I was determined to take him to a hospital, but once we cleared the gates, he started pulling urgently on my arm to get me to look down at him where I held him on the seat. His lips were almost back to normal again and when I pulled his chin gently down, I could see his tongue looking much better, except for a bit of paleness and a small bit of swelling. He gestured weakly at the pen in his throat, but I shook my head.

"No. I'm leaving it alone and letting the doctors take it out." His eyes got wide again and he started struggling to put up his hand and yank it out, but I held his wrist firmly and shook my head. "Sorry, but this time, it's non-negotiable. You need to let them check you out at a hospital." I squeezed his hand when he started to shake. "I promise I won't leave you, but you've been through a lot tonight. This has to be seen by a doctor so they can patch you up. You're under attack by a warlock and I'm not taking any more chances. Relax and let me help you. I'm going to, anyway, whether you want me to or not."

He shook his head violently and tried again to get up, but I put a quick spell on him to hold him immobile. He glared at me with those expressive dark eyes of his, but I wouldn't be moved this time. I spent a minute or two neutralizing the nasty little hex we'd brought with us as Taylor drove us quickly to the nearest ER. Thibeau seethed silently beside me in the seat, lying half across my lap.

When we arrived, Taylor pulled up to the door and ran inside. Within a few seconds, some nurses were beside me with one of those mobile gurneys, and I quickly released my hold on Beau so they could get him on the thing. As angry as I knew he was at me, I saw him looking around for me and I stepped up beside him to hold his hand. He gripped mine tightly, even as he was shooting those death ray looks at me. I smiled reassuringly and walked beside him as they wheeled him into a room. We passed Taylor as he was coming out, and he gave me a nod to tell me he was going to park the car.

In the end we were in the ER for quite a while, with the grim-faced doctors giving me a hard time about my impromptu surgery, and explaining to me how I *wasn't* MacGyver, and how I could have done serious damage to him with the pen, and why the *fuck* hadn't I call 911 or an ambulance and so on and on. And on.

Then when they saw the kind of shape Thibeau's back and hips were in, not to mention the wound only partially healed on the back of his head, it opened up a whole other can of worms. I thought they would call the cops on me then for sure. I had to use some compulsion on them to calm them down.

That's when Thibeau intervened and let them know, through a series of notes, hoarse whispers and head shakes that I hadn't been the one to inflict any of the damages on him. He told them that I was simply a friend he had called for help after he got out of the BDSM club in Tremé. Thibeau had always been a fluent liar, but this time I was glad of it.

One CT scan later to check for a concussion and a lot of dark looks and whispered discussions by the doctors, and they still didn't completely buy our story. But they did call in a social worker, who made me stay outside while she talked to Beau. Of course, some of the welts were partially healed by this time due to my ministrations in the car, so the staff was pretty well convinced I was his abuser, no matter what he said about it, and he was just trying to cover for me.

The social worker gave me an evil look when she walked past me coming out of his room, and I smiled sweetly at her. That went over about as well as you might expect, but with Thibeau steadfastly saying I hadn't touched him and no evidence to prove otherwise, they finally discharged him, and we walked out of the ER a couple of hours later. Taylor was in the waiting room lounging against a wall. He straightened with a look of profound relief when he saw us and led us out to the car.

"Take us to Dauphine Street, Taylor."

Thibeau whipped his head around as well as he was able. "The Quarter? Why on earth are we going there?"

"To stay at my house." He looked at me so blankly, I was surprised. We had spent a lot of time there in the past. Some of the happiest moments of my life, actually. Apparently, not as meaningful to him, though, since he didn't seem to remember.

"My house. On Dauphine Street. You must remember it."

He still had no recognition in his eyes at all. "No," he said, anyway. "Anyway, I'd rather you just took me home, Nic, please. I'll be okay."

"Don't be stupid. You're not going anywhere near that house until I reverse the hex on you. Which you could do yourself if you still had any power." I turned to look at him. "What the hell happened to you, Thibeau? Why are you practically a void?"

He flinched at the word and looked out the window next to him. "I don't want to talk about it."

"Of course, you don't. You've made it obvious over the past two years you don't want to talk to me about anything."

I took a deep breath, willing myself to calm down and not compel him to talk. I could morally and legally as a *législateur* use my power on him and compel him to tell me the truth, but I reminded myself sternly of all he'd been through tonight, dug my fingernails into my palms and told myself I'd regret it if I said or did something harsh right now. I met Taylor's amused gaze in the rear view, and he wisely looked away.

Twenty minutes later, we were pulling up in front of the little house on Dauphine. There had been quite a few changes made since the last time Thibeau had been here with me, and I thought he might mention it. The exterior of the old French Creole cottage was "artfully distressed." Which was some expensive designer's idea of making it look like it hadn't been painted in fifty years or so, with more "distressed" wooden shutters closed over the long French windows in front to make the house look almost derelict.

It was actually gorgeous inside, though, and modern, with an open floor plan, exposed brick walls and black oak floors. There was a loft space up some imported spiral stairs, a master bedroom on the bottom floor and two separate baths. Basically, it had been gutted on the inside and the designer took away all the old-world charm and made it New York modern. I personally wouldn't trade the new rain shower and the Japanese soaking tub for ten times the amount of old-world charm that had been sacrificed, but then I was a Philistine as my mother never tired of telling me.

I saw Beau's eyes widen as we got out of the car and he saw the place, and he glanced over at me warily. I couldn't tell what he was thinking, but if I didn't know better, I'd have sworn he didn't recognize the house at all. When I opened the front door and he stepped past me, however, his mouth dropped open. It did look vastly different from the last time we'd been here. The same designer had been turned loose to redesign the space for me, and she had favored lots of leather, chrome, skylights and cathedral ceilings, as well as Vieux Carré cast iron on the banisters and window interiors. It was ostentatious and over the top, a little like me, so I loved it, staying in it whenever I came to New Orleans on business or to visit Gabriel.

I took Thibeau's arm to lead him over to the leather sofa and deposit him there, then had a few words with Taylor after he carried the luggage in from the car. I had plans for the anonymous hexer and I needed a few things from the shops, especially if I was going to fight fire with fire as I had planned. And I had always been a firm believer in payback.

Since this was New Orleans and the French Quarter, I figured Taylor could find the kind of supplies I'd need no matter how late it was getting, while I got Thibeau into bed and worked on a few wards and charms to keep him safe until morning. If he'd really been kidnapped like he said, I found it alarming to say the least. The attacks on him had been both vicious and nasty, and had intended to kill him, though obviously the last one had been the work of a witch, the attack relying mainly on classic voodoo. However, it had felt stronger, somehow, like a hex on steroids. Like a strange mixture of high magic and voodoo.

"Can I get you anything to eat or drink?" I asked, extra politely—very unlike me, actually. Beau must have thought so too, because he gave me another oddly wary look.

"Just some water, please."

I gave him a bottle of cold water from the refrigerator and held on a second or two longer than I should have as I handed it to him, so he'd look up at me. I managed a pleasant enough look, and almost without being aware of it, my hand reached out and caressed his cheek. He jumped like I'd hit him, but when I kept my hand there, he sighed and leaned into it.

"I'm really tired," he said softly. "Can I just sleep here on this couch?"

"You can take the bedroom. Come on. I need to set up some wards, and you should take some of those pills they gave you at the hospital."

"No pills," he said, shaking his head and pulling away, taking a quick step backward. "I'm okay."

"All right, if you say so. No one's going to force you. But if your head starts hurting or your back, or…"

"I know. I'll tell you if it does. Just let me handle it."

I nodded. Message received. It was none of my concern. I led him toward the bedroom. Meekly he followed me, which was totally unlike the Thibeau I'd known, but like I said, he'd been through a lot this evening so I was trying to cut him some slack. I pulled back the covers and gave him some privacy to undress while I went to look for the candle supply I always kept in the kitchen, along with the other tools of my trade.

I may have practiced high magic, but I knew all about hexes, and I believed in fighting fire with fire. It took me a while to prepare the candles, so he was in bed when I returned, propped up on some pillows with the covers pulled up to his chest. His eyes were still wide open, though he'd begun to droop against the pillows a bit. I thought he was probably a little afraid to relax, and I didn't blame him a bit. I started setting the candles on the floor around him in their glass holders, tearing off strips of wax paper to put beneath them so they wouldn't drip on the new floors.

The candles I used were black, and I'd scratched the word Crossed on each one, with an arrow pointed backward. I closed my eyes when I set them and whispered a spell.

"I send back any hex you send to Thibeau Delessard. I send it back to cross you so none of your works shall prosper. To cross you so that your friends abandon you. So that your enemies always prevail over you. So that your path in life is blocked by misery, pain, and devastation. I send back to you what you send to him."

The candles flared up as I finished and began to burn brighter, their flames all bending in a counter clockwise direction around the bed, as if held in a strong breeze, yet none of them flickered.

"You should be able to sleep safely now. I'll make you a healing potion to drink tomorrow that will help your throat."

"Nic, are my sister and her husband safe, do you think? My brother, Rafe?"

"I think so. All of this has been directed at you so far and no one else. Except for your grandfather, of course. The atmosphere in that house is oppressive but that can't be helped tonight. I need you to start thinking about who has a grudge against your family. One bad enough to warrant killing for it."

His face got even paler. "You think whoever kidnapped and hexed me killed my grandfather?"

"It seems likely. The kidnapper was definitely engaged in killing you when I arrived at the club and would probably have tried to make it look like you were beaten and murdered by some anonymous Dom."

"But why?"

"Why that method? I suppose they thought it might look odd to the police if Delessard bodies kept stacking up at your house."

"No, why kill me at all? And my grandfather for that matter?"

"Who knows? I'll get to the bottom of it, don't worry. You're the head of the Delessard family, so I think whatever the focus is, it's transferred to you. Try to come up with a few names of who it might be."

"That's just it. I can't think of anyone."

"No?" I asked, quirking up an eyebrow. "That's not what the police told me when they came to my office in New York. You gave them my name quickly enough."

"They came to your *office*? *In New York*?"

"Sure did. Told me to keep myself available for possible further questioning."

He put his face in his hands. "I feel awful about it."

"Well, don't worry about it. I'm sure it will pass. Just give it a minute." I turned back to leave and the misery in his voice stopped me cold.

"Nic…"

I sighed, but I didn't turn around. If I looked at him, I'd be lost. "I'm sorry," I said, dropping my forehead against the door instead of banging it the way I wanted to. I hadn't meant to say that while he was still so hurt.

"I shouldn't have said that. I guess we're all a little on edge. Why don't you try to get some rest? I'll be right outside on the couch all night, and we can talk more in the morning."

He nodded and I started out, but again his soft voice caught me again with my hand on the door knob. "Nic," he said.

I blew out a ragged breath. "Yes?"

"Why are you helping me? After…after everything that's happened between us?"

This time I turned to gaze back at him. "It's my job, that's why."

"And all I am to you now is "a job" you have to do?"

"You made it that way, *minou*," I said, and watched his eyes flash angrily at me in the candlelight.

In the old days, I would have known what to do for him when he got like this. He had once been a powerful witch and almost— though never quite—as strong as I was. He was naturally dominant, a force to be reckoned with for his magic and his strength, but inside him, he longed for someone else to have the upper hand. To make him feel their power and force him to submit. As a witch, he had rarely, if ever, found that in any of his lovers, until me. Most had never understood that his need to submit was even greater than his need to dominate. It was vital for him to give up some of that tight, iron-like control of his for the briefest of time, just to be able to survive. But God, how he'd hated to admit it.

The last time I'd forced him to recognize my power over him had been the last night we were together two years ago before I left for New York. He'd been at this very house on Dauphine Street, excited about leaving New Orleans, but nervous and dreading facing his grandfather and leaving his family. He hated to see me leave for New York without him, even though he'd asked me to do that very thing to give him more time to work out his notice at his job. As always, he was a study in contradictions.

He had been restlessly pacing and unable to settle. We'd argued over something minor and ridiculous and he'd gotten so angry, so fast that I had known he was spoiling for a fight. He needed me to quiet his mind and his nerves and make him relax.

I was stronger, both in natural ability and physical strength. I was bigger, taller, with easily twenty-five pounds of muscle on him, so when he'd finally launched himself at me, spitting mad like a cat, I'd caught him in mid-air and thrown him against the wall. I was on him before he could move back into the fight.

"What's matter, minou? Do you need my attention? All you have to do is ask nicely." I licked up the side of his face and nuzzled my nose into the side of his throat. My knee held him pinned up against the wall and my hands were around his wrists. He made the mistake of kicking out against the leg I was standing on to try and thrust me violently away. He was so asking for it.

I staggered back and almost fell, but I regained my balance quickly. We stood glaring at each other from a couple of feet away. Then I smiled at him—a feral smile full of promise. He broke for the front door, but I was standing too close to it, so he changed directions and ran to my bedroom. I followed him at a leisurely pace, then closed the door and leaned against it. He was standing by the bed, looking around wildly for an escape route. I held up my finger and crooked it at him. "Here, kitty, kitty."

He snarled as I stepped forward and then he made the mistake of pulling back his hand to hurl magic at me. I froze his hand in mid-air, picked him up with my own magic and slammed him down on the bed, holding him there. He lay on his back, panting for breath as I fell on him, straddling him to force his wrists into the cuffs and secure them to iron rings on the headboard. Then, when I had him where I wanted him, I stood back up and looked down at him as I began to unbutton my shirt. "What does my kitty need me to do for him?"

"Let me go!" he cried wildly, trying to wrench the cuffs from the frame. The iron prevented him from pulling them free, and I felt his magic try to assault me again, but I threw it off. My own magic was

71

stronger than his. "I hate you!" he shouted and I shook my head, laughing at him.

"Now, baby, you know that's a lie. Tell Daddy what you need."

He made a wordless sound of rage and started to fight, kicking and bucking his hips, trying his best to break the bed and get away, when that was the last thing he needed. I let him exhaust himself for a few minutes, then stepped closer, reaching into my pocket for the switch blade I carried on the streets of the Quarter. I had it, not because I needed it for protection, but mainly for the intimidation factor. I loved to whip it out and use some showy wrist action to make it spring open. What can I say? I was all about the drama.

I saw him watching me, those gorgeous eyes flashing, daring me to use it on him and I stepped over to the bed again. Deliberately, I teased it under his chin for a moment while his eyes went wide and he held perfectly still. I could see the pulse beating hard in his throat. Then I moved it down to his shirt and began flicking off buttons, one by one.

"I hate you," he said breathlessly again, and I smiled.

"No, you don't." I blew him a little kiss.

I took my time and systematically cut off every strip of clothing he wore as he cursed me, even his socks and underwear, just because I could. I teased his skin with the viciously sharp blade, but never applied any pressure at all, because I had no intention of harming so much as a hair on his head. This wasn't about that. This was about showing him who was in charge, and making him like it.

And he liked it fine. His hard, dripping cock was testament to that. I took off the rest of my own clothes at a more leisurely pace. Then I took my time putting on a condom, taking the lube from the drawer and letting him watch me get ready to fuck the meanness out of him. "Stop fighting so hard and stop trying to break my bed. I'll have to spank you if you do."

That made him cry out with rage and buck his hips even harder, kicking out and snarling as I smiled down at him. "So much temper. Behave yourself and I might let you come."

I lay down beside him then, trapping his legs with mine and continued my assault. I took my time, licking and biting and kissing every scrap of skin I could find. I spent a lot of time on his nipples, until he was writhing with need and that's about when the begging started. Music to my ears, but I showed him no mercy. He didn't need me to be sweet and gentle. He didn't want it and would have been furious if I'd tried. He didn't get like this often, but when he did, he needed me to be rough and thorough. He needed me to devour him.

When I finally finished teasing him with my tongue and teeth— and I took my time with that—I spread his legs, opened him wide and slathered lube over his entrance.

"Tell me what you want," I taunted him. He had to tell me, he needed to beg me for it because this was a part of what he needed from me. He had a safeword that he'd never used with me, but he knew it and so did I. All he had to do was say it and I'd let him go.

But that wasn't what he needed and we both knew it. Getting him to admit it—to beg for my domination—was key.

"Beg me, *minou*. Don't keep me waiting."

"Fuck you!" he spat out viciously and I smiled.

"I think we both know who's getting fucked here. Now ask for it, kitty, or I'll tease you all night and still send you home aching in the morning."

He turned his head to the side, his chest heaving up and down. An angry tear rolled slowly from his eye and ran down his cheek, and he'd broken out in a sweat. I wrapped my hand around his dripping cock and slowly squeezed, not enough to help him. Just enough to tease. I pressed my cock to his entrance, just barely putting the tip inside. "I'm waiting, baby. Just say when."

He groaned out my name. "*Nic.*"

"What is it *cher*? Tell me what you want."

"I-I…oh God, I need you to fuck me. Please, Nic. *Please.*"

I rammed my cock into him, plunging deep and hard. He cried out and I pulled back and thrust in again and again, pounding his ass as he cried out for more, deeper, harder. I stretched out over him, my hand on one shoulder for leverage as I hammered into him. His cock was hard and hot, throbbing beneath me, and not only did I feel him come in a hot rush of thick, wet semen between us, but he yelled out my name and little sparks of fire danced around the bed. He clamped down around me and I came hard too, bucking forward into him with a groan. I plastered my lips over his and gave him that most intimate of kisses, where I was buried so deep inside him, it felt like we were almost one flesh.

"Nic?" Beau said, shaking me out of my memory. He was looking at me oddly. "Are you all right?"

"Never better," I replied, shifting my feet to adjust myself a little. Only Beau had the power to make me get so lost in my memories.

"Get some rest, and try not to worry," I told him. "Things will be better in the morning."

I left then before he could say anything else, because I didn't want him to see my arousal and because what else was there to say, really? He'd made his choice long ago, and that was that. Now if I could just get my heart on board, and stop calling him 'minou,' and stop being so goddamned excited at the idea of him sleeping in my bed that my dick was as hard as the rocks in my head, maybe I could get on with my life. I could leave this town after the investigation into Abel's death, and I could leave everyone in it in the past where they belonged. And the possibility of that was so fucking remote, I didn't even try to make myself believe it.

Chapter Four

Thibeau

After Nic left, I lay awake for a long time in the beautiful bedroom, on sheets so smooth and soft they had to have a thread count of a thousand plus, wishing I had the courage to tell Nic what had happened. To explain why I hadn't come to him in New York two years ago. After all, my grandfather was dead. Nothing stood in my way now, except literally a bad head for details, a terrible memory, and a lingering sense of shame that had been branded on my brain, thanks to the not so tender ministrations of Dr. Benedict Tarrant, of St. John's Psychiatric Hospital in upstate New York. Assuming that man had even been a real doctor.

He was a lot of other things—ultra-conservative, homophobic religious zealot and a bigot, chief among them. But an actual physician or psychiatrist? It was iffy as far as I was concerned.

If Nic knew what had happened to me in that hospital and how it had taken so much away from me, he'd no doubt pity me, and God only knew how he'd feel about my grandfather. I wouldn't put it past Nic to dig him up so he could kill him all over again. But it wouldn't matter in the end, because it would still be over between us. He would, with the best intentions in the world, eventually lose interest in me all the same. He'd be kind. Solicitous and apologetic. He'd feel terrible about it all, because he really was a genuinely good person. Nic could be arrogant to the people who knew him and vicious to his enemies, but he still had a strong moral code. It was what made him such a good *législateur*. If he learned what happened to me, he might even try to pretend it didn't change how he felt about me, and he'd stay with me. Because it was the right thing to do. But I didn't want him that way.

I knew a practitioner as powerful as Nic Gaudet would want one of his own kind, someone who could keep up with him and even match his magic. We'd had that once and he'd want it again. Who could blame him?

Witches like Nic, like any *législateur*, invariably made enemies. And they couldn't be worried all the time about someone coming after their weaker partners to get back at them. Powerful witches needed to be with someone who could protect themselves, or else— well, good luck with that. Far better for them to keep away from a committed relationship altogether than to be with a léger or a void like me.

And if he found out about what had really happened…that my grandfather and Nic's own mother had conspired against us to keep us apart two years ago. That when I refused to give Nic up, my grandfather had me kidnapped and taken to a private asylum, run by a religious organization and a director who had known Nic's mother personally. If he'd known that the hospital had been paid for by his own mother? If Nic knew all that, there would be literal hell to pay.

I once had the same magic that sang though Nic's blood and his bones. I knew what it was like to be able to tap into the etheric flow and feel that power surging through me, and know that I could do incredible, magical things. I had been addicted to the feeling it gave me. The feeling of flying, of walking a tightrope without a net. Of being a part of something special, available only to an elite few. It had been incredible, extraordinary…and it had only made the fall that much harder. It was all gone now—burned out of me in that place, like my memory.

In the "recreation" areas of the hospital, the attendants had given us paper and some soft leaded pencils—soft so we wouldn't be tempted to cut our wrists with a sharp number 2, I guess. It was much more likely I'd have used them as weapons against the attendants or against that asshole doctor if I hadn't been so drugged up. But at any rate, when I realized I was forgetting, losing big swaths of my memory, I wrote some things down, and hid the papers under my clothes to take to my room and put them under my mattress. Nic's name, his phone number, his address in New York, some details of how we met. I liked to get them out at night and read them over and over, picturing his face in my mind. I still did, from time to time, just to remind myself it had all been real.

Nic and I first met in Tremé, a neighborhood known by its more formal French name, Faubourg Tremé, in the club known as…hell, I can't remember the name, so I guess that memory didn't stick.

Anyway, that section of New Orleans was a racially mixed neighborhood, and historically important, as it not only had a long

78

history but an important one to New Orleans. For one thing, it contains St. Louis Cemetery No. 1 and the graves of early residents, such as voodoo priestess Marie Laveau. But there were also streets in Tremé where you needed to hide your money in your shoe if you wanted to stand a chance of keeping it. Where it was dangerous to walk down an alley after dark because you never knew what might be hiding there. And the street the club was located on was definitely one of those. And that used to be okay for me, because the farther away I was from my part of town, the better.

I needed to be far enough away so I could be reasonably sure I wouldn't be recognized, but I also needed to be in the kind of club where every man there would know what I was after and some would even be in a position to give it to me. I was always feeling edgy back in those days. I don't even remember why anymore. I was still trying to figure things out, I guess, and learn what to do, not only with the power the magic gave me, but also with this strong attraction I had to being hurt and controlled by someone else. It was an awful dichotomy, being so powerful, but longing for helplessness. It was also one that thrilled and shamed me at the same time.

I needed the person who hurt me to be a strong, Dominant *male*. I needed him to wrap my wrists and ankles in iron so I couldn't escape or use my power and then I needed him to do humiliating, painful things to me. I wanted him to fuck me 'til I begged.

Why? I didn't know. Still don't. Nor did I care. I didn't come to that club to be psychoanalyzed or questioned about my choices. I wanted it rough and I wanted it hard. I controlled my appetites, and indulged them now and again. End of story. Move along people, nothing else to see here. It was my life, and while I wasn't exactly happy, I wasn't miserable either. It worked for me.

On that particular night, however, the pickings were slim. I'd already had most of the Doms in the club but none of them did it for me. I'd been to a few of the more reputable clubs in town, where they had things like rules, and I'd rejected them because there wasn't any excitement there at all. Not for me, anyway. There wasn't any edge. I'd come back to this club, because there was always at least the appearance of something dangerous happening there. I wasn't afraid, because why would I be? I was a practitioner. I could compel a Dom, hurl power at him, work a spell on him, or do any amount of damage to him I wanted to, if I were so inclined. There was no issue of being forced or coerced. I literally had all the power. Even with cuffs on my wrists and ankles, there were ways to manage. The cuffs were only leather, so I could still work a spell. I never allowed myself to be gagged. Working spells was an old form of magic, but effective. Especially if done by a powerful practitioner.

I was with Master John that night, as he liked to call himself, negotiating a scene. A short man, not more than five foot three or so, but vicious with it. John was one of those short men who act more aggressive to compensate for their lack of height. His body was thick, and he had some muscles he'd worked hard on in the gym. He liked to use a big braided bull hide flogger on his partners, and he liked me because he hadn't found my limits yet. He was a sadist, but that was okay with me, and he was perfectly competent, meaning he knew how to use his flogger—the tails went where they should, his wrist action was fluid, and he genuinely liked to inflict pain. You could see it in the glow of his eyes.

We were a match in some ways, because he was a dealer of pain, and I was a willing, even enthusiastic "consumer." That night, however, he wanted to try sounding. He hadn't done it personally, but he'd seen it done a few times and he wanted to try it on me. I didn't really mind, though I didn't much like the idea of him practicing on me. Still, I was more or less mulling it over. So, what was my problem? Why was I hesitating to close the deal?

My wants were well known in this place, as was my availability, my preference for casual encounters and my need for pain. People called me a pain slut and I hated that term. It made me feel like a freak, even in this fucked up company. I wasn't just looking mindlessly for pain. I was looking for the connection too, for the purity of sensation, for the physical openness that gave my mind and body the chance to be transformed, to be both powerful and vulnerable at the same time. And maybe for the feeling that I wasn't always in control—something I rarely felt. Something probably only another practitioner could give me, but I kept hoping.

Then I looked up, and the world tilted on its axis. The man who had just walked in was tall with broad shoulders and a trim waist. Handsome didn't even begin to cover it. He had dark hair and dark blue eyes that sparkled with mischief and danger. I felt the power in him from across the room. The air around him was charged with it. He was wearing black leather like a Dom and he looked around and his eye caught mine. I didn't look down—I wasn't that kind of a sub. He smiled, his eyes registering surprise as he recognized my own power and tipped his head slightly at me—an acknowledgement and acceptance. Game on.

Then he came toward us, pulling up a chair and sitting down uninvited, his eyes boring into mine. John glanced up at him and almost snarled. "Who the fuck are you?"

He never even glanced over at him. "I'm Nic," he said to me, ignoring Master John and looking directly into my eyes. "Who are you, *mon minou*?"

John stood up quickly, so quickly his chair fell over backward. He opened his mouth to yell something, and Nic turned toward him, smiling. "You don't want to do this. You want to go get a drink and relax. Chill out. This sub isn't anybody you want."

Without a word, John turned and left, going toward the bar. Nic turned back to me. "Now, you were saying?"

"Was I?" I lifted one eyebrow at him.

"I think so. You were about to tell me your name. Or I could just keep calling you *minou*. Either way works for me."

I looked him over and raised one eyebrow. "Kitten? Really? Besides, maybe I like anonymous sex."

He laughed, a quick bright laugh that made everyone around him smile to hear it. Within ten minutes he'd led me to a back room. We didn't even bother with the equipment in there. I'd gotten on my knees to suck him off. He held my head with his hands and fucked my mouth with exuberance and flattering eagerness. His cock was big and thick and perfect.

After he'd fucked my mouth, he picked me up in a casual display of his power, which I soon found out was even greater than my own. I later learned he was also a *législateur*. I should have known it sooner, because it was all over him, and he wore it like a suit.

He put me against a wall, my hands over my head, pinned there by his power and my legs wrapped around his waist. He demanded my verbal submission over and over again until I was whimpering with need and then he fucked me mercilessly. And he called me that stupid name again and even made me say it. I hated him.

I loved him, and never wanted that evening to end. Okay, maybe I wasn't actually in love yet, but it didn't take long. Later that morning, as dawn was breaking, we went for beignets and coffee at a small café on Royal Street, just like tourists. We'd been giddy with infatuation, drunk with our power and electrified from the attraction that was buzzing in the air between us. By then, he'd told me his full name and had seemed to know I must be a Delessard, because of my magic. No other families in New Orleans had magic to the extent ours did. I should have been afraid of him. After all, his family was the enemy of mine. But all I'd felt was fascination.

We agreed our names didn't matter and that the old curse couldn't touch us. I had no idea then how wrong we were, or how I'd come to regret its power later on.

Chapter Five

Nic

The curse of the mirrored-box is a very old type of reversing spell used in voodoo traditions to send evil back to its source. The source, in this case was whoever was attempting to work a hex on Thibeau. Even though I'd set the wards, I wanted a little extra insurance.

By the time I left Beau's room and made myself and Taylor a drink, he was walking back in the door with the items I needed to work the spell. He'd found me a small, wooden jewelry box, a plain hand mirror, some glue, twine, and a little voodoo doll, like the ones the tourists bought when they came to visit New Orleans. I already had the hexing candles I'd need, like the ones I'd set up in Thibeau's room.

The type of doll or poppet didn't matter, really, I could have just as easily made it out of cloth or even sticks from the garden. This was just convenient, and readily at hand in any tourist shop in the Quarter. The box could be made of anything, such as a cheap chipboard box like those found in craft stores, a shoebox, or this little jewelry box. I had even known some crafty *législateurs* who made their boxes to resemble tiny coffins. A little too showy for my tastes, though I could appreciate the irony.

HEXXED

A hex was strictly dark magic and could be dangerous if performed by a warlock or a hoodoo or conjure-man. The word warlock literally translated from the Old English as oath breaker. Originally, they were traitors and scoundrels who preyed on innocents to save themselves. When the good Christians of the world began following Church law, some continued to follow the old pagan ways. These people were often called witches, and were hunted down and subjected to painful and humiliating trials followed by horrible murders from burning, drowning and hanging.

The ones who turned in the "witches" to save their own skins, and to make a profit, became known as warlocks. Many of them were actually practitioners of magic themselves, hiding in plain sight and turning in these poor innocent pagans to force the attention of the Church away from themselves. They were often rewarded with the money and belongings of the deceased.

As time went on, these oath breakers weren't satisfied with the paltry income they received from turning in harmless old men and women and they began to strip power from the ether to turn their spells against more prosperous targets. They became so greedy, honest practitioners weren't able to get enough power to do their work or even protect themselves and so had to band together to create the *législateurs*, or the law makers, whose job it was to find these warlocks and punish them for their misdeeds. And that went for any kind of dark magic.

A hex had the power to backfire on the source, if he or she didn't know what they were doing, or even if they did when the person sending back the hex was more powerful. It was forbidden to most practitioners, but I was allowed to punish a hexer, though only after I'd witnessed the provocation firsthand.

While Taylor leaned against the counter, sipping his bourbon and watching me, I quickly constructed the hex. First, I put a cloth over the mirror and broke it with a heavy knife handle from the kitchen drawer. Then I carefully glued the pieces to the inside of the box. I put the doll inside the box, wishing I had some nail clippings or hair from the source to put with it. Instead I pictured that house and its grounds in my mind, because I knew the source had to be there. That's where Thibeau had been attacked twice, so it was only logical.

It was dangerous without a specific target in mind, because if others there were practicing any kind of harmful spells, then they might be affected too. Still, I had to keep Thibeau safe, and I had little patience for warlocks or conjurers who used hexes. And Beau's safety came first.

I bound the box with twine, sealed all the openings with candle wax and placed the curse by saying a spell. "May all the evil you send to others return to you tenfold." The air crackled a little as I said the words, and I used the rest of the hexing candle to burn down over the box as I sipped my own glass of bourbon, sealing the source inside and setting the curse.

"Is that it?" Taylor asked and I shrugged.

"I could have you take it to a graveyard and petition the Baron or some other powerful spirit to keep the source down." I thought it over for a moment. Baron Samedi was a Lwa, pronounced like *lo-a,* or one of the "invisible ones" in voodoo. Witches and sorcerers of voodoo often petitioned him and others like him, but it required payment, and it would kill the source.

"No, I'd rather not do that without a specific name. Let's see what this does first."

"What are you going to do with that box?"

"Take it to a crossroad and put it out. This box will not only turn the curse back on its source, but leave undeniable evidence at the scene where the hex was conjured."

"Well, I'll take it to a crossroad for you and say good night then, boss. I'll be back later, but call me if you need me."

"Will do. Good night, Taylor."

He left and I went back to the bedroom, intending to check on Beau and then bunk down on the couch in the living room for the night. There was a loft upstairs where Taylor was sleeping, but I preferred to be closer to Beau.

As I entered the bedroom, it was dim and the flickering light from the candles lent a soft glow to the man lying on his back on the bed. I'd hoped to steal in quietly and get out again before he noticed me, but his eyes opened as I came in and he leaned up on one elbow and looked at me. He was heartbreakingly beautiful in the candlelight.

"Hi," he said softly.

"Hi, yourself. I was hoping you could rest. You're not in pain, are you? I can get the pills if you are."

"No, I just have a lot on my mind tonight." He took a deep breath. "We need to talk about…" he took a deep breath. "About us. About what happened when I didn't come to New York."

"No, we don't. And there is no us. Not anymore. That's over and best left in the past."

"But Nic…"

"No," I said firmly. That's when he held out a hand to me, and I sighed and moved toward him like a moth to a flame. Self-preservation had never been one of my strong points.

"If you don't want to talk to me, then I'll understand," he said in a soft, hurt voice that stabbed into me like a knife. I sank down beside him, helpless against the tears I saw shining in those eyes. "But I wonder…I wonder if you'd consider making love to me just one more time?"

I think I must have raised both eyebrows or gasped or something, because he continued on in a rush.

"It doesn't have to mean anything," he said, shaking his head before I could draw in

a badly needed breath to answer him. "I know how you feel about me now, and I promise I wouldn't…that is, I won't make more of it than it is. It would be a comfort, that's all. After what's happened. You don't even have to look at me—we could put out the candles and just be here together in the dark. You could pretend that I'm someone else if it would help." He gazed up directly into my eyes. "Please, Nic. Just give me this. One more time."

I sat still for a moment, hardly daring to breathe. But there had to be some honesty between us. I think we owed each other that.

I took his hand in mine and rubbed my thumb over the back of it. "Did you know that I came here to New Orleans to kill you?"

He gasped in shock and tried to pull away, but I held on and shook my head. "Oh, not seriously. I was angry, and it was all bluster. I knew I could never hurt you. But I told myself that stupid lie and I even fantasized about it a little. I thought you'd told the police to suspect me out of pure spite. Out of some kind of need to hurt me, even though I never knew why you called it off in the first place. Called *us* off. Did you know I waited at the airport for you for hours that day two years ago? I thought maybe you'd missed your plane, and I couldn't get you to answer your phone to find out for sure, even though I kept calling and calling. I was worried sick about you."

Thibeau groaned and tears filled his eyes, but that wasn't what I wanted. Not at all. I put a fingertip under his eye to catch a tear as it fell and brought it to my lips. "I promised myself in New York that I'd taste these tears of yours. That was when I was still pretending that I wanted to kill you, and my mind played out one fantasy after another of what I would do to you when I found you. On the way down here, I stared out the window of the plane and planned how I'd hunt you down and hold you captive somewhere. Put you in irons and make you get on your knees and admit you were wrong and maybe put you up against a wall and fuck you until I grew bored with it. That would no doubt take days and days. Weeks, maybe months." I laughed bitterly and shook my head.

"See, the trouble was, I couldn't imagine *ever* getting bored. Not with you, and even in my own mind I couldn't call it fucking—with you it was always making love." I put my face down in his hair and just breathed him in. "I should have known then how much you can still affect me, even if *you* don't feel it anymore." I leaned back to look down at him. "How do you do that by the way, Beau? How do you stop loving somebody when you loved them as much as I did you? I want you to teach me how, because I have no idea."

Thibeau drew in a sharp breath as if my words hurt him. "Please, Nic," he said, his voice miserable. "You don't understand. Don't be angry at me. Just for a little while. Don't spoil this if it's the last time we'll ever make love."

He pushed down the sheet covering him, and I saw that he was naked underneath. He slowly stroked one hand over his gorgeous cock, still desperately trying to hold my gaze, but my eyes had already dropped down to follow his hand without my conscious volition. I was nearly dizzy with desire as I envisioned being inside him, tormenting his prostate as I made him come over and over again until he begged me to stop. I lowered my hand and pressed a fist against my own aching cock and determinedly turned away. I *wouldn't* give in to this.

His hands reached for me and drew me back around. "What is it, Nic? Don't you...don't you want me anymore?"

I looked up in surprise. He had to know I wanted more than anything to make love to him, but I still hesitated. Not just because of what was between us, but because I knew what he'd already been through tonight. Despite everything, I wasn't so selfish that I would put him through even more. He had been severely beaten and desperately hurt. How could I take him now? Because I knew that once I got started with him, it wouldn't be gentle and it wouldn't be fast. I might hurt him without meaning to.

I was shaking with how much I wanted him, but I had to be strong. "What do you want from me, Thibeau?"

"I want you to make love to me," he said, one eyebrow raised. "Was I not being clear enough?" He squeezed my hand. "If you're worried about me being hurt, please don't. I'm feeling much better. Really, I am. You mostly healed my back and he never…he never penetrated me at all."

"There was still trauma."

"I'm not traumatized. Not anymore. And I *want* you to make love to me. I want it so much. Please, Nic. There may not ever be another chance, once you… once I… Well, we do need to talk later and I have some things to tell you. Things you'll want to know, I promise. But right now, I'm telling you that I'm fully aware of what I need. And I need you. Please Nic."

"Why do you suddenly want to make love to me?"

He gave me that old sexy grin. Trouble was, it didn't reach his eyes. "It's not sudden. And it hasn't been so long you've forgotten how good we are together, surely. I've missed you, Nic. What do I have to do to get that across?"

I shook my head. Missed me? Wanted me? Sudden fury reared up to take the place of the heartbreak that was tearing me apart. Beau had known exactly where I was all this time—and I had the restraining order to prove it. All he had to do was pick up the damn phone! Why was he lying about this? I wasn't sure, but I intended to find out. Just as soon as I'd scratched this itch I had. He wanted to make love? Okay, maybe I'd take him up on his offer.

The hard, bitter knot of anger that never seemed to go away in the middle of my chest was aching fiercely. I rubbed at it and looked down at him.

"You missed me, huh? You want me to think about someone else? Maybe it's you who wants to think about somebody else. Okay, turn over then, so you don't have to look at my face." I gave him a little push, trying deliberately to hurt him. "And I don't have to look at yours."

His eyes lit with the vibrant hurt and maybe just a touch of defiance. Good—I could work with that. I didn't want him sweet and vulnerable and compliant. Not the way I was feeling.

"What's the matter? Not romantic enough? Well? I'm waiting. If you want this, turn over and put your face in those pillows. If not, I'll go back out to the living room."

Slowly, with lots of glances up at me from under thick eyelashes, he turned on his side, his pretty cock bouncing around a little as he flopped over. He reached to stroke himself again, but I knocked his hand away. "No. That's mine."

Still lying on his side, he leaned up on one elbow and gave me a look like he used to in the old days. Defiant and challenging. Then he lifted his chin and started lazily stroking himself again, countermanding my order and punching his cock through his fist while he looked directly at me. He knew exactly what that did to me. I pushed his hand away and started to slap his erection with an open hand. I drew back my hand but he flinched, looking scared, and I couldn't do it. I just couldn't. My hand fell to my side, but his erection flagged anyway. Hating myself, I tipped up his chin and made him look me in the eye. "Call me Master."

He blew out a deep breath and then his eyes lit up with a fiery, passionate expression I couldn't quite read. He was turned on by this, the kinky little bastard, and his cock slowly began to thicken again.

"I don't mind calling you Master," he said, in a tone that would have been the same if he'd just called me *darling*. "And I'm sorry, Nic. I never meant to hurt you. I'll call you anything you like. *Mon maîtriser...mon cher...mon coeur.*"

Damn it, I refused to let myself be affected by him like this. By his sweetness. I'd made a big enough fool of myself over him already, and I reminded myself sternly that he was full of lies.

"Turn over, damn it."

I pushed him over, putting his face in the pillows. I may have used a touch of power on him to make him stay put. Maybe a little more than a touch. I drew back my hand again to slap his beautiful ass despite everything, because if I didn't hit something or somebody pretty soon, I felt like I'd die, but somehow in the short distance it took to reach his skin, the slap turned into a caress. My hand skimmed over him with the lightest of touches, and I was mortified to realize my hand was shaking.

How did he keep doing this to me? I stood up and began tearing off my clothes. I fumbled in the drawer beside the bed for a condom and lube, lecturing him the whole time I prepared myself to fuck him.

"You destroyed me once, Thibeau. Did you really think I'd let you do it again? You ran away from me and never looked back. Why? Was your grandfather going to cut you out of the will? Because you were too much of a damn coward to tell him to just fuck off? He wouldn't have liked it if you left. So what? Did he mean so much to you? More than I did? At least admit you never really cared about me. Maybe you were just playing games to dig at old Abel. You lied to me when you said you loved me! That had to be it or else you'd never have left me hanging in New York waiting for you! You hurt me, Beau!" My voice broke in a sob at the end and I was mortified.

"Nic, please," he said, his voice muffled by the pillows. "Oh, God." It was a whimper.

I fell on my knees beside him on the bed, pulled open his ass cheeks and gave his ass a lick from his balls all the way up to his tight hole. He made a sound halfway between a squeal and a whimper, but I showed him no mercy.

"Hold still, damn it," I ordered, and proceeded to fuck his hole with my tongue. After only seconds of this, he was babbling and making incoherent sounds. When the begging started, I finally relented and put my lips up to his ear.

"Is that enough lubrication for you? Do you need more?"

He groaned and I could feel him trying to get up, but I pushed him back down with my power and first bit and then licked one of his ass cheeks. He yelled out something unintelligible again, but his hands still stayed wrapped around the pillows because I was exerting my influence on him to make him think he couldn't break them free. I laughed bitterly, and a long shuddery moan was his only reply.

I slicked myself some more, preparing to take him, because, no matter what I said, I couldn't make myself hurt him. I wet my fingers, then fucked and massaged him for a minute or so, just to make sure he was good and ready. I enjoyed the little sounds he made as I tapped his prostate over and over and made him squirm and writhe. Then when I thought he'd had enough of that, I leaned over him and murmured in his ear. "Get ready."

I guided my cock to his little pink hole, slowly worked in the tip as I held his hips. I intended to thrust hard into him. I fully intended to hurt him this time the way he had hurt me and I meant to make him squeal.

"Say my name, because you're going to scream it in a second or two. You need the practice."

He was silent, still breathing hard, and I had a moment of regret so strong it almost stopped my heart. I felt a sudden unutterable sorrow that it had come to this. That we had taken that bright, sweet spark that was once between us and stamped it out. Then I remembered what I'd been through when he never returned my calls, when he refused to see me and got that restraining order to keep me away from him. It had almost killed me. And I hardened my heart against him again.

I reared back to thrust up and into him, to shove my cock in all the way 'til my balls rested against his delectable ass. But the second I touched him, everything changed. My hard thrust became a long, gentle glide that stroked him all the way in. And once I was inside him, in that sweet, tight heat, I couldn't seem to move. I just lay there in that closest of embraces, shuddering and unable to pull away from him. I began to rock gently against him, feeling completely undone.

"Nic," he said, his voice still muffled. "Please listen to me. I never meant to hurt you. I swear it! You have to let me tell you. I have to explain."

"No!" I couldn't bear to hear his lies, and I'd given him far too many chances already.

I let him up for air then and ripped myself away from him, because despite everything I didn't want him hurt and how pathetic was that? How fucking stupid could I be? He had almost killed me once and now I should let him cry and plead and just go crawling back to him? No! I should let whoever this was in his stupid family hurt him with those hexes and sit back and watch it all burn. I shouldn't have this feeling of awful, lost despair. This feeling in my chest that I would die if I kept on being mean to him. If I didn't kiss him and tell him I loved him, and that I'd never stopped. He turned his head to look back at me and I gazed down at him…and I was lost.

I crushed my lips down on his and kissed him until we were both breathless. His lips were plump and soft as I remembered and his moan of pleasure made me even more excited, and I wouldn't have thought that possible. I was still buried deep inside him, in his soft heat, and my blood was pounding in my ears. He had no right to have this much power over me. He had no right to make me feel so out of control! I ground my lips into his a few seconds longer, and then I pulled away and looked down at him. Those beautiful eyes were wet and glimmering at me in the candlelight and my anger and bitterness dissolved in a whirl of misery. Christ, what was I doing? I loved him. I'd never stopped.

"Please, Nic. I can't take it if you hate me."

"Oh, Christ, Beau. I don't hate you." A tear fell from my eye and splashed down on his shoulder. "*Cher*, damn it, I love you. I never stopped."

I should have left—I should have gotten up and walked out of there to protect myself, but I couldn't seem to make myself move. He said my name again and looked up at me wonderingly, and I fell back on top of him like a man dying of thirst would fall on water. No sane man could have resisted him, and I was far from sane at that moment. I thrust into him again and again, and I felt my orgasm rising in me like a strong wave. "I don't hate you," I groaned and came hard and fast, the orgasm crashing over me and sweeping me along with it. I laid my head on his back and made a strange sound that could have been a sob. The truth of it rang through my soul. "I love you, Beau," I whispered.

I lay there on top of him for a long moment and then I rolled off the side of the bed to dispose of the condom. I knew I should get up and leave, but I just couldn't. Not yet. He turned over too, trying to catch his breath, and held out a hand to me. I lay back down beside him and felt his fingers wrap around mine.

It was then I smelled the smoke. At first, I thought it was from the candles lined up around the bed, but then I realized it was far too thick and cloying to be from any candles. I sat up when I heard the roar and saw a flame roiling out of the fireplace and swirling up toward the ceiling, before turning toward the bed like it knew exactly where we were. The flames on my ward candles blazed up in response, but the mass of fire coming for us was far too strong to put up enough of a defense against it. Red and black and formless, the thing's smoke had the smell of a charnel house. It rose up over us, one tendril of fire leading the way and pointing down like an accusing finger, while we lay there in stunned silence looking up at it. I tried to move and couldn't, feeling as if I were bound in invisible chains. I could only lie there, waiting for the inevitable, when we would burst into flames and be incinerated.

HEXXED

Thibeau made a strangled sound and I shifted my eyes to him, watching a snake-like thread of smoke from the tendril of flame going up his nose, choking him. My God, it was killing him! His whole body was spasming and I called desperately on my power, marshalling a defense from the etheric flow. I tapped into it as much as I dared and concentrated all my efforts on breaking free. Suddenly my paralysis fell away, and I rolled to the floor and raised my hand toward it, crying out, *"Reddam malum!"* Which literally meant, "Repay Evil." It was one of the most effective spells I knew to use against an attack like this.

The smoke streamed back out of Thibeau, but the flame simply froze in mid-air hanging over us for a moment. The heat of it scorched my skin. I felt as if it were waiting to see what would happen next—like it was alive and full of menace. I took a deep breath and called again on my power, but I knew with a sinking feeling, it wouldn't be enough. From beside me, I sensed Thibeau struggling to his knees beside me. His hand reached out and he threaded his fingers in mine. I glanced down at him and nodded. He held on tightly to me and we called out together, *"Reddam malum! Defendat nos a malo!"* Repay Evil. Protect us from evil!

I looked down at Beau and his dark eyes were blazing. I could feel his hand tingling on top of mine. The power flared up inside me, and though it was mostly my own, it had a touch of Thibeau's in it too. I reached farther down into the ether, searching for his old magic and it was there, though diminished and small. Still, what was left of it leapt up to meet my hand and surged into me. It was enough

99

to help me defeat this—I could feel it racing into me and through my bloodstream. We aimed our hands, our fingers entwined, toward the evil that was trying to kill us both and spoke the spell again.

"Reddam malum! Defendat nos a malo!"

The flame and smoke quivered in mid-air for another moment and then seemed to roll back in on itself, becoming a ball that shot backward up the fireplace with a sudden whoosh and a roar. I broke away, pushing Thibeau behind me and went after it, calling out over and over, *"Reddam malum! Reddam malum!"* As the hex flew back up the fireplace and home to its origin, all the fight drained out of me and I sagged down in front of the hearth.

The door was flung open behind me and Taylor burst into the room. He must have come back home while I was making love to Thibeau. He ran toward us, putting his body in front of mine. It was a noble gesture but quite unnecessary. I put my hand on his leg and shook my head. "It's over now. Gone."

"What *was* that?" Thibeau asked from behind me, his voice shaky with fear. He looked scared to death and I didn't blame him. I had never had that much power directed at me before either.

"I don't know, but we have to find out. Whoever is doing this is somehow growing stronger. That was immensely powerful, and I've never felt anything like it before. It was nothing like the previous hexes, which could have been done by any practitioner or even a conjure-man.

"Who the hell is doing this? If there's anyone in the country with that kind of power, I'd know about it."

"What about the box I put out at the crossroad? And the wards you set up around the bed—didn't they help?" Taylor asked.

"They helped or we'd both be dead now. They just didn't help enough." I got to my feet and pulled my trousers back on, then turned to help Thibeau to the side of the bed and pulled a blanket over him. "This thing is strong. Stay inside the ring of candles, Beau, while you get dressed. Then come in the living room. We have to talk."

Chapter Six

Thibeau

Nic's driver brought me a cup of strong tea, along with one of the pills the doctor had given me. I took it in a trembling hand and gave him a sulky look that I couldn't seem to help. I remembered how he'd put himself in front of Nic at the fireplace and I wondered if Nic was fucking him.

My head was splitting and I felt queasy and sick at my stomach. I muttered my thanks, and the man smiled down at me. I felt a vague stirring of memories. I'm sure I must have known him from before, but he was one of those things apparently lost to me forever. He was darkly handsome in a rough trade kind of way, and he had a raspy, kind of growly voice. Very sexy. Though he was being nice to me, I resented him and his closeness to Nic. The closeness Nic used to feel for me.

Nic was pacing around the living room, drinking from a glass of some amber liquid. Whiskey, probably. I saw his hand tremble as he poured himself another glass. He finished it and came to sit down in front of me. His clothes looked disheveled, and his hair was messy from where he'd run his hands through it earlier. His lips were still kiss-swollen and his eyes were cobalt blue with passion. He was gorgeous.

"Who's doing this, Thibeau?"

"I have no idea," I said, looking at him in surprise.

He made a sound of impatience. "It has to be someone you live with in that house. Now stop lying, damn it, and trying to protect them. They certainly aren't trying to save you!"

"I'm not trying to protect anyone either. I really have no idea!"

"Is it your little brother?"

"No! Rafe would never hurt me. And before you ask, it's not Sophie or her husband! Sophie is my sister and she loves me. Her husband…well, he's a léger. He wouldn't have had the power to do what happened in there."

"He would if Sophie helped him."

"No, I said!" I jumped up to my feet and started to storm away, but his man, Taylor, got in front of me blocking my way.

"Sit down, Thibeau," he said, never raising his voice, but I wished I had the power to throw him across the room. Since I didn't and since I really had nowhere to go and was afraid to go back in that room alone anyway, I threw myself back on the couch petulantly and glared at first one of them and then the other. "It's not anyone in my family, I tell you."

"What about the housekeeper and her son?"

"What about them? Camille is in her seventies, and she has no magic. She and her son Emmanuel live on the grounds in the groundskeeper's cottage. Emmanuel's probably close to fifty or so, has never caused a bit of trouble and he doesn't have a speck of magic either."

"Which leads us back to your family."

"It's not any of them, I tell you!"

Nic blew out a breath and I could see him trying to be patient. "All right, calm down. Drink some of your tea or whatever that is and relax a minute." I settled back in the chair, still glaring at him and not pacified in the least. I took the damn tea, drained it all in one go and banged it down on the saucer with a little clatter of china, hoping to break it. I looked back up at him defiantly and saw him smiling at me.

"Feel better?"

"Not really," I replied, tipping up my chin. "I don't like to be pressured by *batons*."

"I'll take it under advisement. Now tell me more about your grandfather's murder. Who found him?"

I sighed heavily, just for show and to irritate him. He used to hate it when I did that. "The police are investigating the crime."

"And so am I. I have jurisdiction over this and you know it. He was a practitioner and subject to our laws. Now answer my questions. Who found him?"

"My brother Rafe, but he just opened the door and saw him on the floor. He came for me right away. I went in and turned him over to check for a pulse."

"Which he didn't have, I assume."

"No, he was already cold. He'd been dead for maybe an hour, the coroner said."

"He was stabbed ten times." Nic glanced over at Taylor, and then back at me. "A bit of overkill, wasn't it? Was there anyone else in the house other than your family?"

"Obviously there was, since *none of them did it*!"

He gave a little sigh. "Describe the scene for me."

"Okay, Sherlock. My grandfather was dead, lying face down on the floor in a pool of blood. No murder weapon that I could see."

"Wait a minute. No murder weapon? What was he stabbed *with*?"

"A knife, one would suppose."

His eyes rose to heaven and his lips twisted a bit. "What kind of knife?"

"I-I don't know. The police didn't say."

"All right. Go on."

"The vault door was open. I went inside to check and found the safe open too. It was empty, so the police think it was a robbery, and my grandfather happened to come in at the wrong time and was killed for it."

"A robbery? Was there any sign of forced entry? A broken window? A jimmied door?"

I flushed. "No. Not that I saw."

"What was in the safe?"

I glanced up at him. "You know what was in there—the De Lys diamond. The blood diamond." It was my family's most valuable possession by far and very old. The stone was over a hundred carats, and rightly belonged in some museum or other and not in our family vault. But it had great significance to the Delessard family, and to the Gaudets for that matter, though I didn't remember exactly why. The rumor in the family—probably apocryphal—was that it had once been a jewel in the crown of some Hindu idol or other. I remembered that little odd bit of trivia, which was the perverse way my mind seemed to work most days. The gem was a rare rusty red color that was called a blood diamond, and had been passed down by one of our ancestors. It had been involved in the cause of the feud, but I didn't remember the details.

"Ah yes, the DeLys diamond," Nic said. "The one your family stole, which started up the feud between the Gaudets and the Delessards."

"So you say. I don't know. That's not what I heard."

"I'll bet."

I'd lied, of course, when I said I'd heard differently. I probably *had*, but I'd forgotten, or had never really paid much attention to all the stories my grandfather had droned on about over dinner some nights. I'd never even seen the stone—only heard stories about it. Occasionally Abel had talked about the stories of the diamond's curse and its origins. Maybe I should have been paying closer attention, considering the course my life had taken. My parents both killed in a car accident when I was young, and then later what happened to me. That had been tragedy on an operatic scale, so maybe there was something to this curse after all.

I must have said some of that last bit out loud because Nic nodded. "Yes, the diamond was rumored to have great power as well as a bad curse on whoever owns it," Nic continued.

"Oh?"

"It was created by a powerful warlock, Jean Claude De Lys in the early 1800s," he said, mostly for Taylor's benefit. But I had forgotten, so it was news to me too. "It became known as the blood diamond, because of its color and because De Lys used the stone in his dark magic." He frowned at me a moment, looking puzzled. "Why do you look like you don't know all this? I know you do, because we've discussed it before."

"Oh," I said, looking bored. "Well, whatever. I guess I forgot."

"The stone is supposed to require a blood sacrifice to unlock its power and protect its owner from the curse," he said, talking to Taylor again, but watching me closely. "According to family lore, it could make the owner powerful beyond imagining. *If* he was willing to kill for it. Members of our two families were already in the order of the *législateurs* at that time and they went after DeLys to get the stone away from him before he destroyed all of us. Beau's great-great-whatever grandfather went rogue, lured by the promise of such power and he stole it. He became the recipient of the stone and all the power of it transferred to him. *My* grandfather killed him for it, but the stone had already gone missing. It was rumored that the Delessard family managed to somehow get it inside their iron vault, but they denied the claim and hid the stone away. No one outside your family has seen it since."

"Is that how the feud between our families started?" I asked, interested despite myself.

He looked at me oddly. "You know it is. Why are you asking me these questions? Years later, the stone turned up in the Delessard family, but by then it was dormant and a decision was made by the *législateurs* to let the family keep it, if they promised to make sure it stayed hidden away and locked up in iron."

"Well, you're right about that. It's been in our vault. And Abel kept it safe and dormant. He wasn't a warlock, you know. He wasn't always a good man, but he didn't practice dark magic. The stone was definitely asleep. I remember that much. But it went missing the night he died. The police did a thorough search through the vault and couldn't find any trace of it or of anything else of value."

"That's the problem," Nic muttered softly. "If whoever stole it killed your grandfather for it, then he's awakened the curse and the new owner is the recipient of the power."

"But power that great would turn that person into a warlock."

"Exactly. And this warlock is trying to kill *you*. Damn it! I knew that attack was too powerful! I mean to find out who's behind it."

"You don't believe in that curse, do you?"

Raising one eyebrow, he looked at me. "Of course. Don't you?"

"I-I don't know."

Nic looked at me oddly then got up to pour himself another drink. Taylor was standing by the small bar cart and Nic leaned in to say something to him softly. They shared a grin and a bolt of jealousy shot through me. Were they laughing at me?

Nic came back to sit down again and continue his interrogation. "What else was in that safe?"

I blinked at him. "I-I don't know for sure. He never let any of us down there. Never showed anything to us."

"I just can't figure out how this murderer has learned all the spells he's been working. Some of them are old ones and truly nasty."

A sudden memory came wriggling back in my brain, though, as I thought about it. Memories had a way sometimes of coming back to me like that when I least expected them. Once as a young teenager, I had found an old book in the library. It had attracted my eye because it was so ancient, the binding almost falling apart in my hands when I took it down to look at it. I loved books and was fascinated by history, so I was curious about this book because it seemed to call to me when I saw it. I felt like it wanted me to hold it in my hands and turn its pages. Abel had come in and seen me with it. He'd looked surprised and had taken it away from me, but very carefully, as if handling a live grenade.

"Where did you get this?"

"On the shelf. It looks really old and I wanted to look at it."

"Not this one, Thibeau," he'd said. "This is a Grimoire. I'll put this back in my vault, shall I? It can be dangerous in the wrong hands."

"What's a Grim...whatever it was you said?"

"A Grimoire is a book of magical spells. But this one is not just any Grimoire. This one is the Rauskinna, a book of evil magic and spells using necromancy, or calling the dead. This book is more terrifying than most of the black magic documents ever written. It was so dark, that most people could not believe it was written by a Christian bishop, but it was. I've always believed he must have been a warlock. He lived in Iceland centuries ago. This book's main objective, he said, was to use magic to gain control of Satan himself." He glanced down at me and shook his head. "It's too valuable to destroy, so I'll just take it away and lock it up, shall I? I have no idea how it came to even be here in our library or who could have left it here."

He went away with it then, and I wiped the hand that had held it absently against my thigh. It felt as if it had left a greasy stain on my jeans, but when I looked down at it, nothing was there. It was the same feeling I got when I stepped into the basement that night after we found Abel's body. The same as the smoke that had gone up my nose in the bedroom earlier. Dark magic.

I told Nic the memory and his eyes narrowed. "The Rauskinna? Are you serious? I haven't heard of that in ages. I thought all copies of it had been destroyed."

"Abel said he would put it in the vault and I guess he did. I never saw it again after that. And it wasn't in there when the police came."

"I see. So whoever stole the diamond might have taken the book too."

"Yeah, I guess so."

"*Merdasse!* Well, that's a fucking disaster. Tell me about the wards your grandfather set up around the vault."

"Just protection wards. Powerful ones. He set them to keep the diamond—and I suppose the Rauskinna—safe."

"What exactly is that, boss?" Taylor asked.

"A Rauskinna is a book of spells collected by a so-called Christian bishop, who was undoubtedly also a warlock. Incredibly evil. It's what's called *maleficium*, which is sorcery or malevolent magic intended to cause harm or death to people or property. It's basically a textbook for a warlock's power."

"The wards my grandfather set in the cellar were worked to keep evil out. They were like magic shields intended to turn away harmful influences. The book was put into an iron vault so it would become dormant too."

"Until someone tried to use it. And it doesn't sound all that dormant if you felt the power when you held it in your hand all those years ago."

"Maybe not then. But after being in an iron vault so long, it would have lost its power, surely." But I remembered the greasy feeling in the cellar when I stepped inside and a shiver ran down my spine. Nic saw it and shook his head.

"No, it wouldn't have. It would have just gone to sleep, like the diamond did. And the murder of your grandfather no doubt woke it up. Books like the Rauskinna crave sacrifice and blood. As for the wards your grandfather set, as you said, wards are intended to keep evil out. They wouldn't have helped if someone were already inside your house…if they were already in the cellar, for example, hiding or waiting there when Abel came down."

That meant he suspected my family, of course, who were the only ones who would have been inside the house at that time of the morning. I opened my mouth to defend them again, and he held up a hand. "I know, I know. Your family would never harm him. But somebody did. Who else had access to the house?"

"It's not exactly a fortress. The *servants*, as you call them come in and out of the house as they needed to. Whenever they needed to. And Abel had visitors from time to time. His doctor came to see him occasionally. Sophie and Christophe and Rafe…all of them sometimes had friends who came over. An occasional repairman or the fucking pizza delivery guy…who knows? If someone wanted in badly enough, it would be possible, I guess. It's a huge, old house. If somebody wanted to hide inside until everybody went to sleep, they'd probably be able to."

Nic stood up. "Then we need to find out what damage was done to the house when we sent back that hex—if any," he said at my sharp regard. "But not until morning, which is…" he glanced down at his watch. "Just a few hours from now. Let's get some rest if we can, and if there aren't any more attacks tonight."

"Do you think there will be?" Taylor asked, looking around at the shadows.

"No. That last one took enormous power. And we managed to make it rebound on the source. I don't think there'll be anything more tonight. We'll talk more in the morning and decide what to do next."

Nic held out a hand to me. "Let's go back to bed. I'm not leaving you alone anymore tonight, just in case."

"Thank you." I took his hand in relief and gratitude and followed him into the bedroom. We were both exhausted so we got ready for bed again quietly. Nic rolled over on his side away from me, after putting out the light. I fell asleep more quickly than I thought possible, and dreamed I was in the library of Ravenwood, a young teenager again and looking for the ancient book. I thought I was dreaming about finding the Rauskinna, but instead another, different book intruded on my sleep.

In my dream, I was looking for spells to practice. A thing that I used to love to do on a rainy afternoon, when other boys my age had no doubt been playing video games. There was one particular shelf in the library where I found most of the old spell books. It was in a dark corner, a small section crammed full of old, ragged-edged books. I used to happily rummage through the books, which were stacked in messy heaps on the shelf with some lying on their sides. Mostly, they weren't the formal spell books kept in my grandfather's private shelves and which were off-limits to us kids. Most of these in the corner looked more like old recipe books, with cheap, yellow paper and no bindings, many of them handwritten in the old flowery style of cursive that had long since gone out of style. I loved reading the old inscriptions, like "The book of Marie Delessard, 1696." Only of course, written in French, *Le livre de Marie Delessard.* This witch had been a member of my family, almost three hundred and fifty years ago. Maybe even one of my long-dead great-grandmothers.

I looked through the pages, smiling at the simple spells to heal the sick, like one that dealt with childbed fever and another for the ague, which I thought was maybe some other kind of fever. I loved the one for a bad nosebleed.

For excessive bleeding at the nose.
Take a few drops of the parties bloud
in herds or in a linen cloth, burne
alltogether: Et fecit.
Pro eodem
Drye a little of the Pacients bloud
on a fireshovel over the fire, blow it
with a Quil into his nostrills.
This seldom or never fayleth.

It was a gentle book of healing spells, written by a woman whose power wasn't a raging river but more of a still pond. I loved to look at the pages and tried to imagine what her life must have been like. There were other books too, some written by male witches, like my grandfather, and giving good, solid advice on things like bringing down the rain during a drought or dealing with crop blight. Some of them had faded sketches to illustrate.

In my dream, it began to grow dark and I knew someone would come looking for me soon. I ran my hand down the side of the pile of books and felt a leather edge. I pulled it out and looked down at it, and there was that smell of rotting leaves again. I opened the book and saw the front page, decorated by hand with painted figures of demons and monsters in writhing poses. The word *Bestiare,* which meant Bestiary, like an old natural history text book, was written on the front in red in a flowing script. I turned the pages slowly, fascinated by the many creatures the artist had portrayed, but surely none of them could be real.

They were all horrible and menacing, looking out the pages at me with faded, jewel-toned eyes and massive teeth. Each one had a name and a description of the evil things it could do, and as I read, the monsters in the book began to *feel* real. A prickling sense of danger came over me, and I felt a presence, like someone there in the room with me, telling me to keep reading. Keep learning about the fantastic beasts and how to call them and make them do your bidding. The room grew stiflingly hot and the air got thick. I was afraid to keep reading and afraid to look away. I had the feeling that if I did, one of those creatures might jump out of the pages and come leaping for my face.

I threw the book down finally and backed away…right into something standing behind me. Whoever or whatever it was carried with them the smell of the crypt. Bony hands clutched at my shoulders as I tried to get away, but they held me fast with a steely grip. I screamed and a skeletal hand closed over my mouth and nose, choking me and shutting off my breath. I wrenched away and opened my mouth to scream but something slithered inside and slid down my throat. I screamed for real then, over and over again, clawing at my throat and the hand covering my mouth.

HEXXED

Chapter Seven

Nic

"Thibeau! *Cher*, wake up! It's only a dream. I have you. Wake up!"

Beau struggled to escape the dream and my restraining arms and came up flailing off the bed. "Wake up. You're having a nightmare."

He sat up, shuddering even with my arms wrapped around him. I leaned my head against his as he struggled to catch his breath. I could feel the rivulets of sweat running down his face. Surely, we hadn't been asleep long. But I'd been so tired I'd fallen asleep almost instantly and slept hard. The sun was peeping through the blinds, so it must have been later than it felt.

"Oh God, oh God," Beau kept saying over and over, as I held him in my arms and murmured what I hoped were soothing words.

Taylor came flying in with his gun drawn, wearing only his underwear.

"It's okay—Thibeau had a bad dream, that's all."

"No wonder, with all the weird shit going on around here," Taylor groused as he turned to leave, scratching his chest. Actually, I wasn't so sure that particular nightmare had been just a reaction to the "weird shit." There was an odd feel to the room, like some malicious spirit had been in there with us, watching us as we slept.

"I'm sorry, but that dream was pretty awful," Thibeau said quietly, still shuddering as Taylor closed the door softly behind him. "The worst dream I ever had and that's saying something."

"You have a lot of bad dreams, do you?"

"Not like that. Nothing like that. But sometimes, yeah. Sometimes I dream about the hospital." He gasped and angled a frightened, slightly shocked look over at me, like he hadn't meant to say that or mention any hospital, but the word had slipped out before he could stop it.

"The hospital? What hospital?"

He looked away and drew in a ragged breath. "Nothing. Never mind. I must still be dreaming."

"Okay," I replied dubiously. "But what hospital were you dreaming about? The one from last night?"

"Yeah, I guess. Just…leave it alone, okay?"

"No, I…"

Taylor knocked on the door and then walked back in holding up my cell phone. I had heard it ringing in the other room where I'd left it a few times already, but thought I'd call whoever it was back in a few minutes once I had this straightened out with Thibeau. Actually, I'd figured it was my brother, Gabriel, since I saw I'd missed a call from him earlier. Taylor handed the phone over to me silently, and as soon as I put it to my ear, I heard my brother shouting at me.

118

"Where the fuck have you been, Nic? The police have been over here looking for you, and I've been calling you for over an hour. Somebody started a fire at Ravenwood during the night and the police think it was you. I guess they found out you're in New Orleans and now they're looking for you."

"A fire at Ravenwood, huh?" I glanced over at Thibeau. "Just like I thought."

Thibeau jumped to his feet with a gasp. "What? Oh my God! How bad was it?"

"To answer both questions," Gabriel said in my ear, obviously having overheard Thibeau. "Yes, a fire and I don't know how bad, but I guess the fire was bad enough they had to call the fire trucks. The police didn't tell me much. The firemen put it out, and there was a little damage, that's all I know. Oh…and the family was worried about Thibeau, because he was missing, along with his car, but I guess that part of the mystery is solved."

"Yeah, obviously he's not missing. He's here with me. Long story, Gabriel, that I'll tell you later. But Thibeau is under attack. Maybe by a warlock or maybe just a very talented conjurer. But whoever this is has tried to kill him three times now. The last time, he went after me too. I need your help."

"You have it. What do you want me to do?"

"Meet me outside Ravenwood in a little over an hour. It will take us that long to get dressed and get out there. I don't want to go back inside those gates without some backup. I'm not sure what we're going to find."

"I'll meet you."

I ended the call and looked up to find Thibeau glaring at me. "An hour! Fuck that! I need to go now. If you won't take me, I'll call for a Lyft or an Uber."

"No, you won't," I said firmly. "Didn't you hear Gabriel say no one was seriously hurt, and there was some damage but not that extensive? We have time get dressed and get some coffee, for God's sake. By all rights, I really shouldn't even allow you to go back there."

"*Allow* me!" Furious, he flung himself toward the bathroom, but I touched him with my magic to get his attention and stop him in his tracks.

"Slow down, damn it!" I said. "I'm a *législateur*, in case you've forgotten. Our word is law to all practitioners and their families, whether you like it or not. Your grandfather always forgot that fact quite conveniently, or rather, ignored it, and he no doubt passed that down to his grandchildren. It's my job to protect you from anyone using dark magic against you, and it's my job to punish the wrongdoer and put a stop to it. You and your family are all under my authority until further notice. Do you understand or do I need to convince you more thoroughly?"

I got up and walked around to face Thibeau, tipping up his chin with one finger. Still unable to move anything but those flashing eyes, he still managed to use *them* pretty effectively.

I sighed and released him with another wave of my hand. "I'm only trying to protect you from whoever in that house wishes to harm you. I think I have a stake in this now too, since they tried to kill me last night as well."

Beau nodded—one short jerk of his head, but I knew the fight was far from over. "I don't know who was responsible for the fire last night," he said. "Or if anybody was, and the fire was just a coincidence." He held up a hand to stop my incredulous protest. "Okay, it would have been a hell of a coincidence, I admit. But promise me you'll keep an open mind about this."

"Of course."

He didn't quite roll his eyes or scoff in my face, but I think it was a near thing.

"Look, go get a shower and get dressed. I haven't even unpacked yet, but feel free to go through my suitcase and get whatever you need. Toiletries and razors are in the bathroom already, and there are new toothbrushes in one of the bottom drawers. I usually leave a few things here in this closet too, so help yourself. Meanwhile, I'm going to grab a quick cup of coffee, which I desperately need after last night, and then when you get through in the bathroom, I'll get dressed and we can go. You can bitch at me all the way over there. Does that sound okay?"

I got another dirty look and he stalked off toward the bathroom, while I went in for the coffee I could smell brewing. Taylor, who was worth every penny I paid him, was pouring me a cup as I came into the kitchen.

"Thanks, I needed this." He'd added a spoonful of sugar and a hint of cream the way I liked it, so I took a big sip of it and leaned back against the counter. "I guess you heard that about the fire at Ravenwood. We weren't exactly keeping our voices down."

"Were you surprised?"

"No, not at all. I'd hoped for a different outcome for Thibeau's sake, but the atmosphere in that place last night was malignant."

Taylor nodded. "I just hope none of his family were involved, but aren't they the only ones who live there?"

"Yes. Them and the servants. I'm afraid one or more of them have to be responsible."

"His own brother and sister, though? Do you think they'd really try to kill him?"

"The lure of power—and a valuable commodity like the blood diamond—are pretty hard to resist, I'm afraid."

"He'll take that hard. Anybody would."

I nodded. "I know. But I need to find out what's going on in that house. And what happened to Thibeau to take his magic. I managed to muster a little vestige of his power last night to defeat the fire sent to destroy us, but it was almost completely gone, and he used to be one of the most powerful practitioners I ever came across. How the hell does that happen?"

"I don't know, boss."

"I mean to find out. There are mysteries in that house and in that family. And I mean to get to the bottom of them."

XXXX

HEXXED

Thibeau

Nic was as good as his word, and we were on the road within the hour, heading toward Ravenwood. I was wearing a pair of his boots, which were a good fit; his jeans, which were a little long on me; and one of his shirts, which was his favorite shade of blue, probably because it matched his eyes. He would never admit that was the reason, but I knew it was true. The shirt had been laundered but still retained a hint of his musky cologne, or maybe that was just my imagination. Hell, I even had to borrow his underwear.

It wasn't that I hadn't worn his clothes before. In the old days, I often spent the night with him and there had been the odd occasion when we got carried away and things were ripped off me...or him, for that matter. I saw him look me over appreciatively when I walked out to the kitchen. He liked seeing me wearing his clothes—that much hadn't changed.

I reminded myself firmly that it was just his possessive nature and not to make too much of it, but after the way he'd made love to me the night before, I had begun to nurture a tiny, treacherous seedling of hope that stubbornly resisted all efforts over the last two years to uproot it. It was stupid and probably hopeless. After all, I'd had to practically beg him to make love to me. Sure, he'd said he loved me—in the heat of the moment. People always said a lot of things they didn't mean when they were about to come. I wasn't about to pin any hopes on that.

I was sure Nic had probably moved on. Maybe even with the sexy man who was his driver. And considering Nic was on his way to interrogate my family, with the idea that one of them had turned warlock, it was doubly stupid of me to think he and I could ever be together again like we were before. A charge of warlockry was serious and might even have deadly consequences, depending on how bad the infractions were.

Neither of us said much on the way through town and on the road out to Ravenwood. I guess both of us were lost in thought, though I had no idea what Nic could be thinking. And as we got closer, I became more and more concerned about what state we might find Ravenwood in, despite Nic's brother Gabriel's assurances. I was afraid there might be extensive damage to the house. What would we do if there was? Any amount of damage might be devastating to us financially. I'm sure Abel had insurance—or did he? Abel had been so arrogant, like all the practitioners who had a great deal of power, that he may have thought he could prevent any disaster from befalling his home and property and therefore didn't need something so mundane as insurance. I was nervously biting one of my cuticles when Nic noticed and pulled my hand down.

"Don't, *minou*. I can feel you fretting all the way over here and it does you no good at all. Don't borrow trouble. Whatever the damage is, you'll be able to handle it."

"I'm not 'fretting.' And it's easy for you to talk. You *have* money."

"Don't you? You and your family have jobs, I assume. You're still a teacher, aren't you?"

I made a noncommittal noise and turned my head to look out the window, avoiding the question. I used to be a teacher, yes. I'd taught history to eleventh graders in a private academy in the city back when he'd known me before. But dates and names now were like slippery eels that slid and slithered away from me if I reached too hard for them. Many of my memories had slowly returned, but not all. Not by a long shot, and it had been well over a year since I returned home. I despaired of ever being as knowledgeable about my facts as I'd been before, and that didn't bode well for my future in a classroom.

"Rafe works," I said, pointedly ignoring his question about my own career. "He's a bartender and makes pretty good money for a guy his age. Especially in tips. And Sophie's been trying to get pregnant. She works from home now, doing accounting on a contractual basis, and she does okay. Her husband is a car salesman at the Ford dealership in Jefferson Parrish. So yeah, we have some money, but not enough to make a lot of costly repairs to the house if there's extensive damage."

Nic gazed at me thoughtfully and I knew he'd noticed I hadn't mentioned my own job.

"Have you been ill, Thibeau?"

Surprised, I whirled to look at him. "Why do you ask?"

"You're pale and you've lost about twenty pounds you didn't need to lose."

"Thanks."

"You know you're beautiful. I didn't mean that. But you're not working now, are you? And you mentioned dreaming about a hospital. What happened to you, Beau?"

He shrugged. "I don't…"

"Want to talk about it. Of course not."

We were almost at the gate of Ravenwood by that time and I saw a black Mercedes convertible parked near the fence. I'd never met Nic's brother Gabriel before, though I'd heard a lot about him. He'd been living in New York back when Nic and I had been together. Taylor pulled up beside the expensive car, and a young guy got out and came around to get in beside Taylor. He was a lot like Nic, which was to say, extraordinarily good looking. Same broad shoulders, black hair and blue eyes. He turned to look back at us after he got in the front seat and smiled at Nic, who grinned back and quickly introduced us.

"This is my brother Gabriel. Gabriel, this is Thibeau."

"Hello, Thibeau, I've heard a lot about you. I was sorry to hear about your grandfather."

"Thank you," I said, automatically, though I didn't really think he *had been* sorry. Still, I supposed it was nice of him to say so.

"The fire department was leaving as I arrived," Gabriel said, directing his comments to Nic again. "But some cop arrived a few minutes ago. A detective I think, wearing plain clothes. He stopped and came over to show me a badge and ask what the fuck I was doing parked out here. I had to use a little compulsion to convince him I wasn't interesting in the least."

"Are the fire investigators still inside?"

"Yes, you've got a nice, full house, I suspect. How are you going to handle this and explain why we're both here?"

"Thibeau will say he's invited us if they ask." He glanced over at me. "That goes for your family too."

"What about the detective?" I asked. "Last week, I told him there was bad blood between our families and I gave them your name as a possible person of interest in my grandfather's murder. Now I'm just going to waltz in there with you? He may not believe it."

"Maybe not, but I can 'convince' him not to ask too many questions and to wrap things up quickly. Your brother and sister will be aware of it when I use compulsion on him, so you'll need to take care of that situation."

"But what about the investigation?"

"We're handling that now," Nic said firmly, in a tone that didn't brook argument.

Taylor drove through the gates and up to the front door. Nic told Taylor to join us inside after he parked, and I took a deep breath and led Nic and Gabriel up the broad steps to the front door. Before I could even get there, the door flew open and Sophie practically flew into my arms.

"Thibeau, we've been so worried!" she said, hugging me tightly. She pulled back and her gaze examined me closely. "I saw that car pull up and then *you* got out! Whose car *is* that? Are you all right?

127

Where have you been all night? Did you hear what happened?" Her gaze traveled beyond me to Nic and Gabriel and she frowned. "Oh my God, what are *they* doing here?"

Her rapid-fire questions were so typically Sophie that I had to smile. She was like a small, yapping puppy sometimes, and especially when she was worried or upset. I loved her dearly, but she could be a bit much. Her husband appeared in the doorway behind her. Christophe was much calmer, though he regarded Nic and Gabriel suspiciously too, before he stepped forward to greet me. I noticed immediately that both of them had angry red burns on their forearms and hands, and my heart sank. The burns had obviously been treated recently and had ointment of some kind glistening on them. One of Sophie's arms was also bandaged, and Christophe had gauze wrapped around his hands.

"I'm okay, Sophie," I said, gently disengaging from her and holding her arms out to the side. "But what's all this? What's happened to you?"

"We had an awful fire in Grandfather's room upstairs. It was in the middle of the night and thank God the fire alarms went off and woke us all up. I got these burns when I tried to put it out, but they're better already." She looked behind her and then whispered to me. "I can work on them when everyone clears out of here. But Rafe said to leave them for now, because he doesn't want to make the investigators wonder about how we got healed up so fast."

I was hyper aware of Nic behind me, near my elbow and listening to her every word. I was feeling extremely protective of her, so I put my arm around her shoulders and drew her back inside.

"Where is Rafe?"

"Right here," he called out as we came inside the house. He was walking into the wide foyer from the front parlor. I saw immediately that he had bandages on both his hands too.

His eyebrows came together immediately when he caught sight of the men following behind me. "What the hell are *they* doing here?" he asked, his tone belligerent as he tipped his chin at them.

"You know why we're here," Nic said smoothly, stepping up beside me. "I told you I'd be back. We should have been called in when you found Abel."

"Better late than never, though, right Nic?" Gabriel said, clapping him on the shoulder. "We're here now to take charge." He smiled at Rafe, though the smile didn't reach his eyes. I got a sudden chill down my spine as I realized what bad enemies the Gaudets could make to our family if they thought my brother and sister had turned warlock.

Gabriel looked around the foyer and made a soft whistling sound. "What's wrong with this place? It feels like it's been stripped." He glanced at Nic. "Even the air feels foul and used up. Almost...oily."

"Yes, there's a warlock operating here."

Rafe bristled and opened his mouth to angrily respond when the detective appeared in the doorway behind him. Detective Arceneau, I remembered, was the one I'd talked to about Nic right after my grandfather's death. I should never have brought up Nic's name at all, of course, but I'd been badly shaken that night after finding Abel's body. In the end it had been really lucky for me that I'd brought Nic's name up, though, because if I hadn't, he might not have come back to New Orleans and then I'd be dead by now.

The detective who was looking our little group over with interest at the moment was probably in his early thirties and tall, with dark brown hair and a piercing gaze that was focused on me and the men behind me.

"Mr. Delessard," he said, nodding at me. "Good to see you all in one piece." He had a bit more than a hint of the Cajun accent that I had always found charming. His name indicated he had a Cajun heritage, too.

"Your brother and sister have been worried about you," Arceneau continued. "And you, Mr. Gaudet, is it? We've been trying to reach you on your cell phone since about two a.m." He looked Nic over challengingly. "What brings you to New Orleans? Interesting timing, by the way. I suppose you can account for your whereabouts last night."

"Do I need to?"

Arceneau narrowed his eyes and I broke in. "He was with me, Detective. All night long."

"I see. And may I ask why you weren't answering your cell phone either, Mr. Delessard?"

"Oh, well, I…" I broke off, suddenly feeling at a loss. Where the hell *was* my phone? And my wallet and all the contents of my pockets for that matter? I couldn't believe I was just now considering the question. That hit on the head must have been worse than I thought. How had the hospital not asked for my ID or at least insurance information? Yet I couldn't recall a single detail.

The detective's eyes were bright with curiosity and suspicion as I hesitated, but before I could come up with an answer, Nic stepped up beside me. "Detective Arceneau, was it?" he said, holding out his hand. "I don't believe we've formally met."

I knew what he was doing, of course. He was riding to my rescue like he always used to do, and besides, I knew that his touching a person made it much easier to compel them.

"Mr. Gaudet," the officer said in acknowledgment. "Might I ask what brings you here this morning?"

"Of course," he said, smiling at the detective. "I'm with Thibeau, and that's all you need to know. You've really gotten all the information you need from here this morning, haven't you? I'm sure you're needed back at your office."

The handsome young detective blinked at him a couple of times and then turned back to Rafe, seeming to be a little confused. "I-I think I have all the information I need, Mr. Delessard, and I…uh…I'm needed back at the office. I'll be back in touch soon."

I noticed Rafe step up protectively beside him and take his arm. His eyes darkened with anger that seemed a little out of proportion. I wondered just how well he knew this man. "I'll see you out, Detective," he said, passing by us with a baleful glare at Nic.

The minute they were out of earshot, I turned on Nic. "Was that absolutely necessary?"

"Yes," he said abruptly and turned back to my sister and Christophe. "How exactly did you come by your injuries, Mr....?

"Decoudreau. Christophe Decoudreau. And I came by them fighting the fire, of course." His tone was pretty defensive. His family were practitioners themselves, though not on the same level as families like ours and the Gaudets. His mother, I believed, considered herself to be a Bokor, which was a Haitian term for a Voodoo witch or sorcerer who worked with both the light and dark arts of magic. He would know what *batons* were and would naturally be a little wary of them, considering his mother was fairly well known in the area for her hexes that she sold in a little shop in the Quarter. They were mostly harmless because she was only a *légere*, like her son, and she did much more business and had more success with her love potions, healing oils and luck candles than she did with any ill wishes or hexes. My grandfather had made sure of that before allowing Christophe to marry his only granddaughter.

"When we came into the room, the drapes had already caught and the flames were licking at the ceiling," Christophe explained.

"And where did the fire start?"

"It looked like it must have come out of the fireplace and out into the room. It sounded like something had caught fire up inside the chimney. I don't think Abel ever used that old fireplace anyway, so it could have been a bird's nest or whatever that caught up. But I don't know who would have had a fire in there in the first place.

Could there have been some kind of spark that set it off? Anyway, when the alarm went off, and we found the fire, I ran to get a fire extinguisher and Sophie used…her own methods."

My sister held up her arms. "Which is how I got these. I stood a little too close to it, trying to hold the fire back. Rafe had come in by that time and he noticed my robe had caught fire. That's how he got injured too. Pulling it off me and putting it out."

"I see," Nic replied. "And no one here had been practicing any spells, I suppose. How convenient."

Sophie looked puzzled. "What do you mean? Do you think *we* started the fire? But why would we?"

"Stop trying to bully my sister," Rafe said, walking back into the foyer, where we were all still standing. His face was furious. "And what was the idea of using compulsion on Detective Arceneau? He's more welcome here than you and your family!" He raked Gabriel with his gaze as well. Gabriel returned his regard with a cool expression, but something crackled in the air between them, and Rafe's eyes got wide. He balled up his fists, and I think he would have started something if I hadn't stepped in between them.

"Stop it, Rafe. They have every right to be here and ask questions. You know that!"

Rafe glared at me. "What are you doing with them, Beau? Especially with this one. Were you really with him last night? We were worried sick about you and all the time you were with *him*?" He asked incredulously and gave Nic a little of the look he'd given Gabriel.

Nic smiled at him, which only made things about ten times worse. His face flamed red. "After all you put Thibeau through, you have a lot of nerve showing up here," Rafe said. "Have you compelled Thibeau too? Is that why he's just going along with all this?"

"Rafe! Calm down and let's go into the front room so we can sit down and act civilized. I know Abel didn't think much of the Gaudets and all the *batons,* but that was *his* issue and had nothing to do with us or any of this. We don't have any choice but to talk with them and you know it."

I took his arm and he didn't pull away, though he gave Nic and Gabriel another defiant look as we went into one of the two parlors at the front of the house. This was the one we used the most when visitors came, and I walked in and sat down on one of the stiff chairs by the fireplace.

"Christophe," I said, "could you ask Camille and Emmanuel to come in here to speak with them too? Tell Camille there's no sense in resisting this. They'll make them come anyway."

Christophe nodded and headed for the kitchen. The rest of us sat down on the sofas that faced each other. Nic and Gabriel stood near the hearth.

I stayed quiet, waiting for Nic to begin his questioning or whatever it was he intended to do, but Rafe was more impatient. "*Were* you with him all night, Thibeau? The police found your car in a parking lot in Tremé, and we had it towed here to the house. What were you thinking?"

Before I could reply, Nic spoke over me. "He was probably thinking he needed to try to stay alive."

Rafe's eyes widened as Sophie gasped. "*What?*"

Christophe came back in the room with Emmanuel following him. "Camille had already left for a prayer circle at her church, but I found Emmanuel."

Christophe sat down beside Sophie, but Emmanuel remained by the door, leaning against the wall. Emmanuel gave both Nic and Gabriel a sullen glare before dropping his gaze.

Nic continued talking as if there hadn't been any interruption. "Your brother was hit on the back of the head and kidnapped right here on this property yesterday afternoon when he went outside to get in his car. He was taken to a disreputable club in Tremé where someone drugged him and then tried to kill him. I don't suppose any of you would know anything about that, would you?"

Sophie softly gasped and Rafe turned to me in shock. "What is he talking about? Beau, you were attacked? *Kidnapped?*"

"I'm all right. Really, I'm fine now."

"He wasn't, though," Nic interrupted smoothly. "He was almost beaten to death and would have been if I hadn't intervened. The perpetrator got away while I was helping Thibeau, but the outcome could have been extremely bad. Then when my driver and I brought him back over to this house at his insistence, he was attacked again by a nasty hex left under his bed that once again had the intention of taking his life." Nic turned to Emmanuel. "I assume your mother cleans under the beds from time to time."

I flushed in embarrassment. Camille was in her seventies and no longer did the cleaning. Each of us cleaned our own rooms, and we had a lady that came in once a week for the heavier cleaning. Camille only did the laundry and some of the cooking these days.

I explained that to Nic and he gave me a speculative look. "I see. So, it could be that no one has checked under the bed in a while."

"Probably not," I said, giving him a dirty look.

"I don't understand *any* of this!" Rafe said, his face strained and angry. "Who could have done something like that to Beau?"

"That's what we're here to find out," Nic said. "Thibeau was attacked again after I got him out of here to a safe location and this time, I sent the hex back to its source. It happened to be a fire hex."

Sophie gasped and her hand flew to her throat. Christophe put an arm around her angrily. "Surely you're not suggesting that one of us would have sent a spell after him to kill him! Are you crazy?"

"His brother or sister are powerful practitioners…and you practice voodoo. Isn't that right, Mr. Decoudreau?"

"I'd never attack anybody in this family!" he shouted. "Don't be ridiculous."

He turned toward Emmanuel. "And you, Mr….?"

"Dubois," Emmanuel answered, keeping his eyes on the floor.

"Mr. Dubois, thank you. I can't help but notice that everyone here is injured except for you."

"That's right."

"Why is that?"

"We didn't hear any alarms over at our house. We didn't know about the fire until the trucks came."

"I see."

Someone cleared his throat behind us, and we all turned to see Taylor in the doorway. "Everything in control here, boss?"

"Everything's fine, Taylor. I was just about to speak to each member of Thibeau's family separately to find out more about the fire."

Christophe shot Nic a resentful look, muttering, "I don't see why that's necessary."

Rafe flopped down beside them, folding his arms. "I don't know what you want us to say. We certainly had nothing to do with hurting Beau." He looked over at me. "Beau, surely, *you* know that."

"Of course, I do," I said, shooting Nic a look. And if looks could kill, he'd have been on the floor at my feet, severely wounded at the very least. "I think *everyone* needs to just calm down."

"Thibeau, can you tell us what happened to you at least?" Sophie looked up from Christophe's shoulder and sniffled. "Did you say yesterday afternoon? I went upstairs to our room after the funeral and I didn't see or hear a thing."

"She took some pills the doctor gave her," Christophe explained. "Then we both lay down and took a nap. I'm sorry, Thibeau. We never heard anything."

"It's all right. It wasn't your fault."

"And you, Mr. Dubois? Did you hear or see anything?"

"No. We had already left by then."

"To go where?"

"To the church. They have Bingo on Friday nights. My mother likes to go and I drive her."

"Ah. All right, then. I assume the people at your church can corroborate that."

"Do what?"

"The people at the church can back you up if they need to."

"Why not?"

Nic smiled. "Why not, indeed. Thank you, Mr. Dubois. We won't keep you further."

Emmanuel left, giving Nic a long, unfriendly look.

"What about you?" Gabriel asked Rafe. "What's your story?"

"I don't have a 'story,'" Rafe said, snapping his gaze back at Gabriel. "If you mean, where was I, I guess I'd left by that time to go out with some friends."

"And will these friends be able to provide you with an alibi?"

"If I need one, yes." Another crackle of energy as they swapped snarls, until Nic put a stop to it by standing up.

"I believe it might be best if *I* spoke to Rafe about his experience with the fire, actually. Gabriel, if you'd do the honors with Sophie?"

"I'd like to go with my wife," Christophe said, half rising, but Nic shook his head and waved his hand at him.

"No," he said, and Christophe fell back on the sofa, looking surprised.

The short, rude answer seemed to startle Christophe, and he glanced over at me helplessly. "I can't get up, Beau."

138

"It's fine, Christophe. I'll go with her, if that's okay with Gabriel."

"Actually, no, Thibeau. I'd prefer you to stay here with Taylor and Christophe," Nic said. Without waiting for my reply, he stood up and motioned for Rafe. "The fire investigators are finishing up their work and about to come down soon to speak to you. As the owner of the property, you need to be here. Come with me, please, Rafe, and you can show me where you and I can talk privately while Thibeau deals with that."

I didn't question how he knew what the fire investigators were doing on the second floor, just like I didn't question anything he could do. He was immensely powerful and always had been. He swept out of the room, not waiting to see if Rafe, who looked like he was about to explode, would follow him. In the old days I could have sent my brother a little calming energy, but now all I could do was hope for the best. He gave me a look as he slowly followed Nic from the room.

I smiled encouragingly over at Christophe, who seemed to be a little worried. "She'll be fine," I said and he nodded like he didn't really believe me.

About ten uncomfortable minutes later, the fire investigators indeed came by to tell me they were leaving. They informed me they had to run some tests, but they hadn't reached any conclusions yet about the fire's origin, and they'd be in touch.

Gabriel came to the door and asked Christophe to join him and Sophie. Christophe rushed past us quickly, obviously anxious to see her. I hadn't heard any loud voices coming from the other parlor where Nic had taken Rafe, so I counted that as a win. And since this was my own damn house and Nic hadn't specifically told me not to leave this room, I got up after another ten minutes of waiting and walked toward the door.

"I'm going up to my room," I told Taylor uncompromisingly and he nodded. "If Nic wants me to stay with him at his house in the Quarter…"

"He does."

"Then I'll need to pack some clothes. And do you have any idea about my wallet and cell phone? What might have happened to them?"

"I don't, no. We can look around outside before we leave. Near the area where you were attacked, I guess."

"By the way, how did the hospital even treat me without insurance information?"

"Nic paid for everything upfront."

Tightlipped, I nodded and started past him only to have him fall in behind me. "I have to go with you," he said. "But I'll stand outside your door."

"Thanks." No sense getting mad at Taylor, I told myself, in one of the mercurial changes of heart I'd been experiencing since Nic came back in my life. But he was only doing what he'd been told, just like the rest of us. I nodded and he trailed along behind me as we went up the stairs. As good as his word, he waited by my door while I went in. I took a small duffle from my closet and filled it with items from my drawers, then headed into the bathroom to get the rest of what I needed. From my closet I took a few pairs of jeans, some shirts and shoes, and then just sat on the bed, wondering what the fuck I was doing.

All this was useless after all. My whole life was useless, really, and it was time to admit it and do something about it. How had I gone on this way as long as I had?

I couldn't pretend the prospect of spending more time with Nic hadn't felt exciting to me at first, but at the same time, I knew the inevitable misery and letdown would come when he went back to his life in New York, and I went back to mine here in this house. It was going to be awful. Maybe as tempting as it was to go with Nic back to that beautiful little house on Dauphine Street, I should make a clean break. Just end it. We'd had our little interlude. Our one for the road, so to speak. It was great sex, but it had to be goodbye sex, which I guess we needed, because we'd never had the chance to have a proper goodbye. He'd told me he loved me, yes. But people said all kinds of things during sex that they didn't mean. I had no doubt it brought back memories and maybe he did love those. But he didn't *love* me. Not anymore. How could he? Too much time had passed and we had missed our chance.

Gloom settled over me like a shroud. Of course. It was so obvious I wondered how I hadn't realized it before. It was over now, and I had to face that and do the right thing. I had to kill myself, because there was nothing left for me except the shame I would bring to my family and the ones who loved me. Rafe and Sophie could and would give me protection but I'd only be a burden to them. It would be best to simply end it all. Just remove myself from the world.

I must have sat there for ten more minutes sunk in the deepest misery I'd ever experienced in my life. I had just got to my feet, intending to go over to the curtains to unhook the cord that held the heavy draperies back, thinking I could fashion a noose pretty easily from it and hang myself in the bathroom. Then there was a quick rap on my door, and Nic walked in. He glanced around for a moment before getting a startled look on his face and sniffing the air. He took a quick and alarmed step toward me, holding up his hand, like he was scanning me. He got almost close enough to touch me and then reeled backward a step.

"Good God. I got here just in time. You were about to hang yourself!"

"I-I…" I tipped my face down to my chest in shame and degradation. "It's for the best, Nic. I need to get out of everyone's way."

"The hell you say!" He looked around and spotted my bag. He took me firmly by the arm. "Good, I see you're ready to go. We're out of here."

I pulled back and tried to get away. "No, Nic, it's no use. Don't you see?"

"No, I certainly do not!"

He opened the door and shoved me toward a surprised Taylor. "Take him downstairs and out of this fucking house. Someone's trying to get him to kill himself."

"What? Boss, I had no idea. He was so quiet in there. "

"Yes, I know. It's my fault. I should have warned you not to let him out of your sight in this mausoleum. Just get him out of here and keep him out. Use force if necessary."

"Hey!" I yelled at him. "Leave me alone—*please!* I know what I'm doing!"

"No, you don't. Take him out, Taylor, while I take a look around."

"You got it." Taylor took me by the arm and looked down at me. "I don't want to have to make you move, Thibeau. But we're going down those stairs and out to the car. One way or the other."

I glared at him and tried to pull away, but his grip was like steel. "Damn all of you!"

He took my arm and began dragging me down the stairs. We passed a surprised looking Rafe as he was heading through the foyer toward the kitchen, and startled, he held a hand up in the air to stop Taylor. But Gabriel walked out behind him and pulled his arm sharply down.

"What's going on, Taylor?"

"The boss told me to take him out. He was trying to kill himself."

"What?" Rafe yelled and tried to run toward me, but again, Gabriel froze him with a single pass of his hand.

"No. Let's wait and talk to Nic. Taylor has him under control for now."

I wanted to kill all of them. "Get him off me, Rafe! Why are you just standing there? Help me! Oh, goddamn all of you!" I tried to turn out of Taylor's grip, but he twisted my arm up behind my back and pushed me roughly outside and down the steps, then pinned me with his body against the side of the car as I tried to get away.

I was spitting mad by this time, but with Taylor's heavy weight against me, I was stuck like a bug on flypaper. I was struggling for breath and managed to get one leg free to kick my foot back and try to do some damage. Taylor simply moved with me, recapturing my leg and pinning me down again. I drew in a deep breath to shout for Nic—to tell him to get his big gorilla off me—and suddenly, the oppression lifted off me and I was free.

It was so quick, so unexpected that I would have sagged to the ground if Taylor's body hadn't been holding me up. I let my head fall forward to rest on the top of the car, and Taylor peered down at me.

"Feeling better?"

"I don't know, I…" I took another breath of fresh air as the embarrassment washed over me. Suddenly, I remembered everything. I knew I had been talking about killing myself, and I knew why. I remembered how simple it seemed—just take the rope off the curtains and hang myself. But though it seemed so clear to me before why it was so necessary to end everything, now it just seemed foolish.

"Oh my God, I was going to do it, wasn't I? I was going to kill myself."

"Beau?" Rafe came up beside me and put a hand on the back of my neck. "Are you okay?"

"I think so. Now. But something came over me while I was upstairs. I never felt anything like that before." I put my hand up to hide my face.

Taylor stepped back from me and let Rafe come closer to put his arms around my shoulders. "Should we call a doctor?"

"No need," Nic said, coming down the front steps. "I found the poppet." He was holding a little voodoo doll in his hand, along with my hairbrush. The little doll was made of cloth and not too big. About the size of my hand. The poppet's eyes were two little dark brown buttons and its mouth was sewn shut. A noose made of yarn was tightened fiercely around its neck, and tied in the yarn were some dark strands of hair.

"It was under your bed again."

Rafe reached for it, but Nic held it away. "No, don't touch it."

"At least take that yarn off its neck."

"No, not until we can anoint it with holy oil. After that, I'll destroy it. I found a hairbrush you left behind upstairs too and brought it with me. The warlock was using your hair to make his or her spells."

I didn't know what to say to that, and I still didn't feel well. Nic put me in the car and stood talking for a few more minutes before joining me in the back seat. Taylor got behind the wheel and we drove back toward Dauphine Street.

Chapter Eight

Nic

I left Thibeau alone on the way home and busied myself with some emails about business I needed to take care of. He needed time to calm down, and I needed time to think. I had the holy oil that I needed to neutralize the poppet. I had an entire bottle of oil, blessed by a voodoo priest, at home with my supplies. I could perform a spell myself, but using the oil was faster and more of a sure thing.

I put my arm around Thibeau and drew his unresisting body toward me, settling him against me. My mind went back to the strange conversation I'd had with his brother Rafe during our talk. In fact, I'd been coming up to confront Beau about it when I found him about to hang himself.

Rafe had been reluctant at first to even speak to me—it was written all over his face when we sat down together. I sat across from him and probed his memories of the night before for a few moments. I found some images of him working at his job as a bartender, like Beau had told me. Some flirting with customers to get better tips and some more flirting just because the guys were good looking. The details he'd provided about fighting the fire were accurate, and I was satisfied he had nothing to do with the attacks on his brother. As a matter of fact, he'd seemed worried sick about Thibeau, so I asked him why.

"What's this concern you have for your brother? It's more than just the natural worry over the attacks."

"I don't want him disappearing again," he said, giving me a resentful look. "The last time he got mixed up with you, everything changed. He went away and came back completely different. He was sick for a long time. I don't want to see that happen. Not again."

"What do you mean? What happened to him?"

"He was gone for almost six months after you left to go to New York. He disappeared the same day you left, and my grandfather said he had to get away to clear his head, but I knew you had something to do with it. You broke up with him, didn't you? After he made plans to go to you? He told me he was leaving and swore me to secrecy. But you told him not to come or whatever and broke his heart, didn't you? That's why he was so devastated that he had to leave."

I clenched my hands tightly to keep from throttling him. "Where did he go? Answer me quickly."

"I don't know. Abel wouldn't tell me. But when he came back, his magic was gone and he was..."

"What? What was he?"

"Broken."

"What the fuck do you mean?"

Rafe turned a stormy gaze on me. "Broken! Messed up! His magic was gone and he'd lost probably twenty pounds and he was pale and he had headaches and he couldn't eat…. God, it was awful. He looked like he was dying. I tried to get him to talk to me but he wouldn't. He used to sit and stare at some pieces of paper he carried around in his wallet, when he thought no one was looking. So, one night when he went to take a shower, I sneaked into his room to take a look at what he kept staring at. It was a little scrap of paper with your name on it, and your address in New York. I don't know what you did to him, but you won't get another chance at it if I have anything to say about it."

I wanted to shake him for more information, but I knew he was telling me the truth. "I never hurt your brother, Rafe. I wouldn't. And not coming to me in New York was his decision, not mine."

"Bullshit."

He looked at me like he hated me, but I couldn't help that. I needed to talk to Thibeau. And I meant to get the whole story, if it killed both of us.

We rode home to Dauphine Street mostly in silence and after we arrived, I immediately put the doll in a glass dish and then poured the holy oil over it, completely soaking it. Then I put it out on the patio until I could burn it and asked Taylor to order us some late lunch. He called and placed the order, while Beau puttered around the bedroom, putting away his things. He glanced nervously at me from time to time, because I sat in the room and watched him, strangely unwilling to have him out of my sight.

Lunch arrived and we sat down in the kitchen to eat. I had ordered some seafood, since I knew shrimp and oysters used to be his favorites, but he only picked at his food, saying he had a slight headache when I asked.

"So… Did the fire investigators tell you anything important?" I asked him.

"No, they said they weren't through yet and would send in their report when they finished their tests." A strand of his hair had fallen over on his forehead, and I wanted badly to brush it out of the way.

"How was your talk with Rafe?" he asked.

"Fine. He didn't want to tell me anything, but he finally came around. I'm satisfied he had nothing to do with it."

Relief washed over his face. "Oh good. I knew he didn't. What about Sophie and Christophe?"

"Things there were not quite as clear, according to what Gabriel told me."

"What do you mean?" he asked, bristling.

"They didn't attack you, but they were hiding something. Something significant. When Gabriel probed for it, Sophie got very angry and protective, and she threw up wards over both their memories so Gabriel couldn't access them."

"Well, I-I'm sure there's an explanation."

"Mm. Gabriel has given her some warnings and now we'll give her some time to think about the consequences of not being entirely forthcoming with a *législateur*. We'll go back and speak to her tomorrow."

"I insist on being there," he said firmly.

"No one's going to hurt her, Beau. She's not a warlock as far as we can tell and there was no sign she'd practiced any of the dark arts. We only want her and her husband to tell us whatever we need to know. They're hiding something, and we may have to persuade them more strongly."

"Not without me being there, you don't."

I may have rolled my eyes a little. "You wouldn't like it, and you won't be allowed to interfere."

"I don't have to like it. I just have to be there with her."

"We'll see," I finally said. "Now, I looked for your housekeeper again before we left. I have a question for her if I can talk to her. Any idea where she might have gone?"

"She goes to her church a lot—hers and her son, Emmanuel."

"His truck was gone too. Where do you think he might have gone?"

"I have no idea. Shopping, maybe? Emmanuel goes sometimes to help. Camille's elderly."

"Yes, that point has been made several times. We can talk to them both again later, I suppose."

He shrugged and I put a hand over his. "You look tired and we didn't get much sleep last night."

"Maybe it would be best for me to just go to a hotel."

"No."

"Just hear me out."

"No. You're about to tell me that you've changed your mind about staying at my house. That you'd thought it over and it would be best if Rafe and Sophie looked after you at home, because they're family, after all, and you trust them implicitly. But if I won't agree to that, then you'll just go to a hotel. And it's best for us—for you, really—not to be around me anymore. It will be harder when the inevitable time comes for me to go back home and leave you behind." I stood up and looked down at him. "To which I call bullshit."

"What do you mean? Do you deny it?"

"As a matter of fact, yes, I do." I held up my fingers and began ticking them off. "You're not safe at home, and surely even you can see that now. And it's not 'best' for you to be away from me. This relationship is actually a long way from being over, and we both found that out last night. I told you at one point that there was no 'us' anymore. That we were over and what was between us was best left in the past. I was lying to you and kidding myself. If nothing else, I've learned that I'm not even close to being over you, and that I'm going to get to the bottom of what happened if it kills me. I don't want to force you or compel you to stay with me, but make no mistake about it, I will if I have to, for your own safety. Now, please. I really don't want to fight you over this."

He sighed and stood up beside me, looking partly pleased by what I'd said and partly resentful of my bossiness. He sailed out of the room ahead of me to express his irritation with me, but I stopped him at the door.

"By the way, your sister and her husband have been confined to their room for a few hours to think things over."

Startled, he turned to glare at me. "Don't look at me like that. They have everything they need, and they'll be allowed to come out this afternoon. Consider this a time out."

"They're not children!"

"They're acting like it, though. Thibeau, I mean to find out the secrets in that house and find out who the warlock is. Do I make myself clear?"

"Crystal," he snapped and went back to the bedroom to flop down on the bed. I had told him earlier he couldn't close the door, so he turned over on his side away from me.

I had a quiet word with Taylor and told him to make himself scarce for a while, and I'd call him if I needed him. Then I went in to sit on the bed beside Thibeau. He opened his eyes when he felt me sit down behind him and quirked an eyebrow.

"Was there something else you wanted to say?"

"I was actually hoping there was something you wanted to tell me."

"I don't know what you mean."

"Rafe told me one of the reasons he doesn't like me is because he thinks I'm going to hurt you and make you go away again."

He flushed and opened his mouth, but nothing came out. "I don't want to discuss this right now."

"Tough shit, because we're going to. Where did you go, Thibeau? After you decided not to come to me. What happened to you to make you lose your magic?"

He flinched and tried to get up but I held him in place. "Tell me, Beau. I think I have the right to know."

"Why?" he cried out, turning to his back to look up at me. "It won't change anything, and I don't want your pity!"

"Beau. Talk to me."

"I was going to tell you, but you didn't want to hear. And you were right! What good will it do? So you can forgive me for not coming to you in New York, right? But at what price? You'll be sorry I told you—you'll hate what happened to me and maybe want revenge, but what possible good will that do now? I still won't have *you,* and I won't have my magic either! It won't ever be the same again, don't you see?"

He tried to fling himself off the bed again, but I caught him and held on. I knew what to do for him when he got like this, but it had been a long time. I'd thought we were done with all of that, but if he needed it again…if it would help him, then I had to do it to make him talk to me.

"Thibeau, get your clothes off."

"What?"

"I think you heard me. You'll do as I say until further notice. Is that agreeable to you? Look at me." He glanced up at me sullenly and met my gaze. "I asked you a question. Be sure of your answer."

He was breathing hard. So hard his chest visibly rose and fell with each intake and exhale of breath. He began to get flushed and sweaty, and I thought for a moment he'd refuse. But then he dropped his gaze and nodded.

"No, I want to hear you. Say the words for me. If you don't want this, then I leave this room, and you can take your nap."

He hesitated for only a moment this time. "It's agreeable," he said with a long sigh. "I guess it's finally time you knew what happened, but I think you'll have to make me say the words." He looked up at me from under his eyelashes. "Sir."

"Get your clothes off and then get back on the bed on your knees."

For a moment I thought he wasn't going to do it, but then with several smoldering looks at me and a lot more little sighs and hesitations, he swung his legs over the bed and began to pull off his shirt. His hands were shaking as he stood and slipped off his pants and then turned back to look at me defiantly. He had been the brattiest sub I'd ever met back when we were together and I'd loved every moment of it. But sometimes when we needed to have a serious discussion, this had been the only way to pin him down— quite literally. Of course, he didn't have much of his power left anymore, but I still wanted that connection we used to have. The deepest I'd ever had with anyone.

He was still hesitating, so after I reached for the lube, I folded my arms and gave him a stern look. "Get on the bed on your knees. Don't make me keep repeating myself."

He knelt on the bed facing the headboard and I took off my clothes and knelt behind him. I pulled him back flush with my chest and began stroking his pretty cock to a leaking arousal. When he began panting for breath and I knew he was about to come, I stopped, pushed him down so his face was in the covers and spent some time stroking his ass. Penetrating him with a slick finger, I slid in and out slowly and then found his prostate. He moaned and I slapped his ass. "Quiet. Don't say a word until I tell you to and then when I do, you're going to keep talking until I tell you to stop."

He moaned again and I spanked him a few times with one hand while I worked his prostate over with the other. "Be quiet, I told you! Not one sound!"

I began to stroke him again. As soon as he started to tremble and groan, I moved my hand up to work on his nipples. I pinched and rubbed them until he was whimpering. Then I bent him over and spanked him for making noises.

He was trembling and had his hands fisted in the covers when I finally pulled him back up against me and began to stroke his cock again. I brought him to a state of trembling arousal before I pushed him back down again. He was so hard and frustrated by this time, he had to be aching for it.

I put on a condom and slicked myself up, easing the tip of my cock inside him and then thrusting in hard to bury it toe-curlingly deep. He groaned out loud and started begging me to move, to *do* something. He squirmed and writhed on the end of my cock. I bit his neck and then laved it with my tongue. I kept kissing his jaw and his ear until I had him in a state of aching, pleading arousal and then I finally went back to slowly stroking his cock, but never enough to let him come.

"Please, *please*, Nic. *Master! Please!*" he begged me and I relented.

"If you want it so much, minou, then come in my hand."

I had stopped stroking him so he had to work for it as I held him tightly in my grip. He thrust his hips back and forth, straining against first my fist and then back onto my cock, which provided him double pleasure, though you'd have thought I was killing him from the moans. Finally, he cried out and came hard, shuddering through an epic climax and then several little aftershocks. When he finally subsided, my dick still hard inside him, I sat back on my heels, pulled him down in my lap and gave him a little nudge.

"Tell me now," I said. "Start talking about the day you were supposed to meet me in New York. Tell me while we're together like this and I'm buried deep inside you. So deep that it's hard to tell where I end and you begin."

He shuddered and sighed. "Nic, *please*. I can't. It-it's a long story."

"I've got nothing but time," I said, stroking his cock again. It was painful to him so soon after his orgasm, and it registered on me that I was being impatient with him when all I wanted to do was soothe him and kiss him all over. I wasn't angry at him. I was simply overcome with emotion. I wanted to hold him and tell him how much I loved him, but first I had to find out what had happened to him two years ago. I had a feeling it was going to kill me when I learned about it, but I still had to find out. I took a deep breath and kept stroking, waiting for him to start.

HEXXED

Glancing at the clock by the bed, I saw that it was three-thirty in the afternoon. It hadn't even been twenty-four hours since I'd seen him again after two long years, but in some ways, it felt like it had been twenty years. Wasn't that always the way it was in the old fairy tales and legends? People fell asleep and woke up the next morning to find twenty years had passed while they lay there sleeping. Or was it a hundred? Either way seemed to work. I felt groggy, like I was trapped in some crazy dream.

A little over two years before, Thibeau and I had decided to run away to New York together. It had all been very Romeo and Juliet-like. A whirlwind romance between two young lovers, two families who hated each other and were in a feud that had lasted a few hundred years. We knew our being together wouldn't be a popular decision. Not least of all because Thibeau's grandfather hated the fact that he was gay. But we were in love and decided the feud was stupid and old fashioned. We didn't give a damn about it or about who did or didn't approve of our love.

My dad had passed away the year before and left me in charge of running the businesses, but by the time I'd met Beau, I already knew I'd have to move to New York. I had two younger brothers to help me. Gabriel in New Orleans and my other brother, Remy, who lived in London. But my mother was insisting I leave New Orleans and go on up to New York immediately, so I talked Thibeau into going with me. Into leaving his home in New Orleans and moving in with me. I'd wanted to marry him.

On the day he was supposed to arrive, I went to the airport to meet him with a ring, but he never got off the plane. The airline said he'd never claimed his seat, and he wouldn't answer his phone no matter how many times I tried to call him. I got an email the next day from Thibeau breaking up with me. Over the next few days, I tried desperately to get in touch with him and finally went back down to New Orleans to find him and talk to him. I wanted him to tell me in person what was wrong. Why he'd changed his mind, because I couldn't believe it.

I was met at the gate of Ravenwood by old Abel himself and told to stay away. When I insisted that he let me see Beau, he called the police, and I was made to leave and later served with a restraining order. I didn't give up though. Not at first. And not for a long time. Maybe six months or so later, I got a letter—an actual letter in the mail from Thibeau. That should have been a warning sign, because who sends letters through the mail anymore? He said he didn't love me, had never loved me. Everything he'd ever told me—every promise he'd ever made—had been lies. He asked me to leave him alone. It was brief and brutal and broke my heart all over again. So, I stopped trying to reach him. For two long years.

I moved inside Thibeau a little, thrusting up even deeper and he moaned. His head flopped back on my shoulder and I whispered in his ear. "Go ahead," I said. "Tell me what happened two years ago. You're not getting out of this."

I thought about how he'd wanted to talk to me the night before, but I'd turned him down flat. I was ashamed of the way I'd treated him then. I wanted desperately to make it up to him. Thibeau was trembling, but he nodded.

"Okay, I'll try. But just hear me out and don't-don't say anything, okay? I'll tell it as fast as I can."

I nuzzled my face down against the back of his neck. "Whenever you're ready."

"The day I left to go to the airport, to meet you," he said, so softly I had to strain to hear him, "I tried to sneak out, but Abel found me with my suitcase and there was a terrible argument. He said if I tried to leave the house to go to you, he'd have me locked up. He said he knew about the BDSM clubs I went to, which was proof, he said, that I was crazy. He showed me the commitment papers. I tried to run, but he caught me—he was so strong, even though he was an old man. I think…and I don't know for sure, but I think he had been playing around with the diamond. I don't know of anything else that could have made him so powerful. He forced a hypodermic needle in my arm, and I woke up in a-a kind of hospital."

I shut my eyes, awash in pain. I didn't want to hear what came next, but I knew I had to hear it.

"It was a private psychiatric asylum. Supposed to be based on religion. And they drugged me so I couldn't use my magic. I was bound to a table and had ice, heat and electricity applied to my body parts while I was forced to watch films of gay men holding hands, hugging and having sex. I was supposed to associate those images with the pain and humiliation I was feeling, and once and for all turn into a straight man. They did this so-called aversion therapy on me at first, and when I didn't respond the way they thought I should, they gave me shock therapy."

I must have made some tortured sound because he reached back absently to pat me, trying to offer *me* comfort.

"Electroconvulsive Therapy, they called it, to get me to admit my sexual preference was abnormal and something I wanted to change. They kept at me all the time. Kept giving me the treatments until I told them whatever they wanted to hear. My 'illness' was being gay. My 'psychosis' was that I liked having other men control me in the bedroom. I admitted I liked men to use whips and chains on me to make me fly. I admitted it and the doctor stepped up the treatments. He explained they were for my own good. He said that one day, I'd thank them. It took me a little over six months to get out of that place. By that time, my magic had been burned away."

"Jesus, Thibeau," I said, my throat so clogged now with tears I could barely breathe. "I didn't know. I had no idea!"

"I know you didn't. I know how my grandfather lied to you, made you think I didn't want you anymore." He turned his head slightly to look around at me. "If you could…if you could just see past this… I meant what I said. I don't want you to pity me. I don't, Nic. It would be ideal if we could go back to the way things used to be now that Abel's gone, but I know you've probably moved on with someone else by now, and I don't blame you. I know I'm not anybody you need anymore."

"Thibeau, there's never been anyone but you. There never will be. *Cher*, why didn't you tell me once you left that fucking place? I'm not accusing you. I just-I just need to know why. Did Abel threaten you?"

"He didn't threaten me. He threatened Rafe, my little brother. He said he'd send him to the same place as he sent me if I left and went to you. He said he had the money to do it. He said…this time he'd tell the doctor to do a lobotomy." He glanced quickly over his shoulder at me and shook his head. "I'm so sorry, Nic. He said he could do it because he had access to plenty of money, and he'd rather have his grandsons dead or 'fixed' than have them be gay. It scared me the first time he said that. I thought he meant to castrate me. Hell, maybe that would have come next. He said he could get all the money he needed for it from…from your mother."

I wasn't sure I'd heard him at first. Then shock, and cold, blind fury rushed through me so hard and fast I felt like I was caught up in a maelstrom, but I tried to hold it together. I could fall apart later but right now I had to hear this. "Wait a minute. Wait a minute," I said, my voice shaking. "What did you say? *My mother* was involved? You said *my mother*?"

"Yes, Nic. I'm sorry. She was the one who paid for the hospital. My grandfather wouldn't have had the money to do it otherwise. They hated each other, but they formed some kind of unholy alliance. She didn't want you to be involved in a homosexual relationship either. Especially with a Delessard."

I couldn't speak. I had no idea what to say anyway. I felt frozen, afraid of what he might tell me next. How the fuck could she? How could she do that to him? To both of us?

"The attendants at the asylum drugged me, so I couldn't use my magic to protect myself, and then they used electricity to induce seizures. Electro Convulsive Therapy. The treatments I'd received weren't actually painful except for the headaches and the jaw aches afterward. But the treatments were so *hungry*, Nic. They ate up my magic along with my memories."

He dropped his head on his chest then and his shoulders shook. I couldn't stand it another second. I withdrew from him and pulled him around into my arms to face me. "Beau, don't. Please don't!"

"I was still luckier than some of the others," he said, sobbing onto my chest. "Some of the older patients in that place had been lobotomized years ago. They put an ice pick in their brains, Nic. Just for being gay. They had been there for a long time, and I used to see them sitting in their rooms staring at the walls or shuffling down the hall. They were lost. Every one of them. I was afraid each time they came for me that they would do something like that to me too."

"Oh, God, don't even say it." I crushed him to me. I held him as tightly as I could, just rocking him in my arms and we grieved together. For what he'd lost and could never get back again, for all the other lost ones too, and for how our own families, the people who were supposed to love us the most, had almost destroyed us.

"I want details on that place. Not right now, but when you feel better. I'll see to it that hellhole is destroyed."

He nodded and we continued to cling to each other. I don't know how long we stayed there like that. Long enough that I heard Taylor come back in and go upstairs to his room. Finally, I shook Beau gently and we went to take a long shower together and then went out to the living room to find something to eat, still in our robes. Taylor came down and made us omelets and we carried our plates to the sofa and put on some mindless adventure movie or other. It didn't matter, really. We only wanted to be together and the noise and the light of the TV soothed us and kept us from being alone with our thoughts. I didn't want to think about things right then. I knew it would all hit me soon—especially my mother's role in this. There would be a reckoning, but I needed to calm down before I dealt with it.

Around midnight, Thibeau fell asleep in my arms, so I pulled a blanket down off the back of the couch and decided we'd just sleep there together the rest of the night. There hadn't been any more attacks, and I took that to mean that either the warlock had learned his lesson and would leave Thibeau alone or he or she had been too badly hurt by our counterattack to retaliate. Either way, I hoped for a more peaceful night. I had a feeling it might be the last one I'd get for a while.

Chapter Nine

Thibeau

The next morning, Gabriel came over and Nic took him outside on the patio to speak to him. I understood it was probably about their mother, and Nic didn't want to upset me by talking about it in front of me. And since it was *about* me and what had happened, I knew I didn't want to hear it anyway. Now that I'd finally told Nic what had happened, I wanted to shove it all in the past where it belonged. I knew that wasn't practical. I'd have to tell my story at least once more to Rafe and Sophie since Rafe had said they were worried about me and since it wasn't fair to keep it from them. If it destroyed the love they might still feel for our grandfather—well, that couldn't be helped. Abel had done a pretty good job of doing that all by himself.

Gabriel left after about a half an hour, with a long look at me. He looked upset and distraught, and I knew Nic had told him what happened two years ago and no doubt had some things to say about their mother. After a few more minutes passed, Nic came back in and poured himself another cup of coffee.

"Want some?" he asked.

I shook my head. "No thanks."

164

He came to sit beside me at the bar, dropping a kiss on my cheek. "Are you okay?"

"I'm fine. How about you after that conversation with your brother?"

He sighed. "About like you'd expect. I told him I want her out of the penthouse in New York. I don't much care where she goes, but I want it to be far away and out of my sight."

I began fiddling with my empty cup. "She's your mother, Nic."

"Not anymore." His voice was so hard and unforgiving, I was a little shocked. I had known he had this steel inside him, but it had never been directed toward me, and I was suddenly very glad. He'd had training as a *baton* to make harsh and uncompromising decisions, even if they concerned his own personal life. Apparently, he'd learned those lessons very well.

"I'm sorry."

"She's the one who should be sorry." He sighed, and took my hand, rubbing a thumb across the back of it. "She's never approved of what she calls my 'life choices,' but she's gone too far this time. What she did to you was unconscionable. Criminal. If it had been only me...but it wasn't. To drag you into that struggle and make you suffer—that's just intolerable. I've made it more than clear to her over the years that she doesn't get to make decisions about my life. My father spoiled her badly, I think, and left her with too much money and time at her disposal. I promised him I'd see to it she was taken care of. I will, but I won't be the one doing it. And she'll be on an allowance from now on, that my brothers will oversee. Gabriel

165

didn't like it, but I'm the head of our family and what I say goes. He can explain to her that I never want to see her again and she's not to make any attempt to contact either you or me or I'll cut her off completely."

"Nic, I don't want to be the cause of trouble between you and your mother."

"You weren't. She brought this all on herself. My biggest regret is that Abel Delessard is already dead. I would have taken a lot of pleasure in killing him for what he did to you and for what he put you through."

"Nic, this isn't what I wanted to happen. I told you that you'd be sorry I told you. I knew you'd want revenge, but that doesn't do either of us any good."

"I know," he said, bringing my hand to his lips. "But you were wrong when you said that if you told me, you wouldn't have *me* anymore. And that it wouldn't be the same. I never stopped wanting you and I never will. I hope you still feel the same way about us, because we're not over. I'm so damn sorry for the things I said to you—for the way I accused you. But I was just reacting out of hurt. I thought you didn't come to me back then, because you'd decided you didn't love me anymore."

"I know, and you don't have to apologize. I should have told you as soon as I got home and trusted you to protect my brother. My only excuse is that I was still pretty indoctrinated and traumatized by all that had happened. I felt a lot of shame. Then later, I thought it was too late."

Nic rubbed a hand over his face, his eyes devastated. "I wish I could make this up to you. Get your magic back for you."

"But you can't, and I've accepted it." I gave him a little smile. "Mostly."

"There might be a way to help you get some of it back. When the fire came for us, I felt your magic still in the ether. Like a little bit of it was still stored there somehow and it responded to me. I used it, actually, to help us. I think a wand might help you. Many of us use one and they help. It's worth a try."

I shrugged. "If you like."

"I do," he said, kissing my fingers again. "I'll find one for you and prepare it myself. I don't want you to worry about anything anymore. Let me take care of you for now."

I pulled my hand away, shaking my head. "I don't need anyone taking care of me."

"But…you lost your job, didn't you? You didn't say, but I suspected, and if you were gone for all that time, I know they wouldn't have held your position for you. Please, Beau, it's the least my family can do."

"I'll find another job. Now that Abel's not around to force me into some marriage."

"What?"

"It's a long story, but basically he wanted me to marry a woman of his choosing and get him grandchildren. I refused and he got angry and made threats."

He looked at me with determination, his mind made up. "If you marry anybody, it's going to be me."

I shook my head. "Now you're just being crazy."

"Why is it crazy? It's what we wanted two years ago."

"But there's been a lot of water under the bridge since then. I need time. You do too."

"Time for what?"

"To consider all that's happened. That's *still* happening. I have a warlock after me, you may recall."

"All the more reason to take you to New York with me and keep you safe."

"And this is exactly what I *didn't* want!"

"Wait—what?"

"You trying to 'keep me safe.' Wrapping me up like a porcelain doll in some spell or other to protect me. I'll fight whoever's after me right alongside you."

He pulled me around to face him. "Beau, the person who killed your grandfather woke up the curse of the blood diamond with Abel's murder and is probably using the Rauskinna to make his spells. Whether he did this on purpose or if he killed Abel and stumbled onto the book, it doesn't matter. You know how evil that thing is. The killer is learning and there's literally no telling what this warlock is going to be able to do soon."

"What do you mean? What can he do?"

"Who can say? So far, it's only been hexes—nasty ones meant to harm. He's already a murderer, and the fact that he stabbed Abel ten times means it may have been done out of rage. But the curse will make this person into someone capable of great evil. He's only testing his power now, but soon he or she might be almost unstoppable. It all depends on how much power they had to start with. In the old days, it took the combined forces of your family and mine to defeat De Lys and make the curse dormant again. I've put my brothers on notice that they may have to help me fight this thing."

"And we can help too. Sophie and Rafe are powerful. Even Taylor and Christophe can help some, since they're *légers*."

"Maybe. But we have to find the warlock first. And by that time, he may be too strong. And I'm sorry, but I still believe the warlock might *be* one of your family members."

I pulled away angrily and got to my feet. "Damn it, Nic, I told you it wasn't any of them! Why would they do such a thing? I had more reason to hate Abel than any of them, and it never occurred to me to kill him."

"Motive can be important, but it doesn't mean everything because it's different for each person. What might make you kill someone might not be the same for another person. You see this in the news every day. It's often more about means and opportunity. And I go by one solid axiom—everybody lies."

"That's ridiculous."

"No, it's human nature."

We glared at each other for a moment—that is, I glared while he gazed serenely back at me. Then Nic's phone rang as we stood there, neither of us willing to back down. In the old days, we used to have arguments all the time. Fights about what Nic called my reckless behavior at the clubs I went to, before he made me stop going altogether or about telling my grandfather all about us. They usually ended with me held up against a wall, being fucked to within an inch of my life, but this fight wasn't like the ones we used to have back then. This one was about my family, my brother and sister, and I wasn't going to give in.

Exasperated, Nic answered the phone and then held it out to me. "Your brother."

I took the phone and turned my back on him, because I knew it would irritate him. "Hi Rafe, *Ça va?*"

"We got a package delivered to the house a little while ago, Beau. I think you need to see it. I guess you should bring the *baton* with you."

"What is it?"

"I'm not sure. A hex of some kind, for sure. It feels malicious. And Gaudet said to let him know if anything else happened."

"You touched it? Shit, hold on a second." I put the phone away from my mouth and told Nic what he'd said.

"Tell him not to touch it again and to go scrub his hands. Stay away from it until we get there."

"Did you hear that?" I said, holding the receiver back to my ear.

"Yeah, okay." He hung up without another word, probably irritated that I was still staying with Nic. It looked like we had to have that talk about things sooner rather than later.

Taylor drove us out to Ravenwood. It was a beautiful day, humid as hell, but that was business as usual for New Orleans. Still, we put the windows down and let the warm wind hit us in the face. It was nice, except for the growing sense of urgency that made me so uneasy and the fact there was a little smell of the swamp in the air, like stagnant water. The gates were open when we got there, so we pulled right in and up to the steps. Rafe came and opened the door when he heard the car drive up. He looked like he hadn't been out of bed long, but he stood back and motioned us inside. There on a table in the foyer, was a small, innocuous looking box. It was wrapped in brown paper and still securely taped.

"Did you wash your hands after you touched it?" Nic said, looking down at it. "This is a hex all right, and sometimes when someone sends one like this, they put poison on the packaging."

"What?" I took a backward step in alarm, and grabbed Rafe's arm to look at his hands. "Did you scrub them?"

Rafe pulled away from me. "Yes, okay? Chill out, Thibeau."

"But you did pick it up?"

"Just long enough to bring it in. *C'est tout.*"

"He should be okay then," Nic said, touching the small of my back. "Calm down."

I hated it when people told me to calm down. It never helped and only annoyed me. I folded my arms across my chest and nodded toward the package. "How do you know what it is without looking inside it?"

"I can feel it."

171

"I can't feel anything." Except that wasn't exactly true. I was getting a sense of something unpleasant in the room, a feeling like something was wrong. "Ugh. I think I see what you mean. What is that?"

"I'm not sure," Nic said. He muttered a few words over the package in Latin, then took out a handkerchief to hold the package down and his pocket knife to cut through the tape and the paper. The small box he revealed was made of thin pine wood. I could smell it when he pulled it out, a musty earthen smell overlaid with a smell like a pine cleanser. On top of the box was a crudely drawn picture of a man sitting on a throne. He wore a black top hat, a black suit, and was smoking a cigar. His eyes were covered by impenetrable black sunglasses.

"Baron Samedi," Nic said, and I glanced over at him, puzzled. "Someone is sending the dead." He glanced back at Taylor, standing behind us. "Get that blanket out of the car, please, Taylor."

He nodded and went back outside, while I leaned forward to look at the box.

"What? Sending the dead? Is that voodoo stuff?"

He nodded. "Yes. The man in the picture is known as Baron Samedi, the Lord of the Graveyard. His name literally means Saturday, the one day that Christ was really, truly dead; the day between the crucifixion on Friday and resurrection on Sunday."

"Well, that's creepy as fuck," Rafe said. "Sacrilegious too."

"Not in the voodoo tradition. Somebody has invoked the Baron to put you on notice." He opened the box and looked inside, poking around with his knife blade.

"What? What does that mean?"

He opened the lid back farther to show me it was full of black dirt and little rocks. "Someone wants a person in this house dead. This is graveyard dirt. A warlock or conjurer who wants to send the dead goes to the cemetery at midnight to invoke Baron Samedi, the god of the graveyard, with offerings of food for the Baron. The Baron then possesses the warlock. Or that's the belief. At the cemetery, the warlock gathers a handful of graveyard earth for the person he wishes to see killed. Sometimes he also spreads the dirt on the paths taken by the victim or victims. Or the warlock takes a stone from the cemetery, which magically transforms itself into an entity, ready to do its master's bidding."

"This is crazy."

"It's voodoo, and don't discount it. These 'sending the dead' spells can make the victim grow thin, stop eating, and eventually die. Or they can open up the possibility in the person's mind of something coming to kill the person in some other way. Think of it as a warning that death is coming. Like I said, this box has just put somebody on notice."

"What?" I asked, grabbing Nic's arm. "Who?"

"It depends. Who here believes in voodoo? The critical factor in a hex death like this one is belief. Belief not just in the hex, but in the power of the Baron. If a person believes that a warlock can make him die by invoking the Baron and then cursing him or crossing him, he probably will die, and no amount of Western conventional medicine can save him."

"Christophe's mother is a voodoo priestess or something, isn't she, Beau?" Rafe asked.

I shrugged. "She claims to be a Bokor or a witch, but I'm not so sure about that part. Let's just say, I'm skeptical. She has a little shop in the Quarter where she sells potions, oils and candles to tourists. Along with some poppets and hexes to be used in her voodoo rituals. They're harmless enough."

"But Christophe believes in the stuff?"

"Maybe. I think so, yes."

"Interesting." Nic glanced back over at Rafe. "Was there a name on the box?"

"No."

Taylor came back inside the foyer with a small blanket and stood beside Nic. He was accompanied by Gabriel. I looked at him in surprise and then back at Nic.

"Gabriel still has questions for Sophie and Christophe, you may remember. I sent him a text before we left."

"I see." My tone may have been a touch frosty, since Nic glanced over at me and gave me a little smile.

"Now—we were looking for a name in the box," he said, and dipped his knife back in the dirt to move it around again. Soon he unearthed a tightly folded scrap of paper. He opened it and looked down at it grimly. "Christophe." He showed me the paper and I saw the name printed there in a childish script.

"Okay," Nic said. "We probably need to take it away before Christophe sees it and then send this thing back to its source."

"Before I see what?" Christophe said, coming down the stairs. "Were you talking about me?"

"It's nothing, Christophe," I said quickly, moving to stand in front of the package. "Someone's idea of a joke. Come on in the dining room and let's have some coffee, okay?"

Thankfully, he came along with me, with only a quick glance over his shoulder at Nic and Gabriel. But Nic had already wrapped the box in the blanket he took from the car and had handed it to Taylor, who took it outside.

"What kind of joke?" Christophe asked, and Rafe came to my rescue. He flopped down in a chair at the dining room table.

"Just one of my friends playing a prank on me, that's all. Where's Sophie?"

"She's coming. She got pretty upset yesterday about being locked in our room." He gave Gabriel a dark look as he sat down beside Rafe. Nic had followed us into the dining room too and stood near the door.

"I hope she's prepared to stop playing games then," Gabriel replied. "Why don't you tell us what Sophie was trying to hide yesterday? Why did she throw up wards around you?"

Christophe's face got red and he shook his head. "I-I don't…"

"Leave him alone," Sophie said, coming in. "You and your brother should pick on someone who can fight back. Someone like me."

"Sophie, be quiet," I said, a little too loudly. I was alarmed because she had no idea what Nic and Gabriel could do. "Go get some coffee and meet us in the front parlor. We need to get this straightened out."

I stood up and went to Nic. He was still and tense, gazing after Sophie with speculation on his face. "Please Nic. This has all been a lot for her. She was really close to Abel and she took his murder hard. Can we just go into the parlor and talk about this? You're always telling me to calm down, so now maybe you could take your own advice? Please?"

Thankfully, Nic nodded and came with me. Gabriel followed us. I hadn't been a hundred percent sure either of them would. We sat down and waited. I was nervous and fidgety, but Nic took my hand and brought it to his lips.

"Don't be so nervous. We're not going to hurt your sister. She's not a warlock as far as I can tell. Though this damn house is so oppressive and stripped that it's hard to get a good reading on anything or anyone. I think she may be covering for someone."

"For Christophe, you mean."

"Maybe," Gabriel replied. "Then too, I suppose it's possible she could be covering for you or Rafe for that matter."

My mouth dropped open a little and Nic gave Gabriel a sideways look that made Gabriel shrug. "No one is above suspicion, brother.

176

From what you told me, Thibeau would have had good reason to hate the old man that much."

"So would I, but I didn't do it," Nic said dryly, and squeezed my hand. "My brother is a stickler for the law, Beau. What he forgets is that if Abel weren't already dead, I'd have saved someone the trouble and killed him myself."

Gabriel gave him a look, and I noticed that Nic saying he wanted to kill Abel too for what he'd done to me still wasn't exactly a leap to my defense. I pulled my hand away from his and he cut his eyes over at me.

Sophie came into the room with Christophe and they sat down stiffly across from us. She gave me a betrayed little look, and I leaned toward her. "Sophie, don't play games with them. If either of you knows anything, you have to tell them."

She looked nervous, chewing on her bottom lip for a moment. "I don't trust them. I don't understand how you can."

Nic sighed impatiently. "We don't have time for all this. Either tell us what you know or I'll compel you."

"You can't compel *me*!"

He must have touched her with his power then, because she gave him a startled look and her eyes got wide. She glanced frantically at me for help. I touched Nic's arm. "Nic, please. Stop and she'll tell you what you want to know. Won't you, Sophie?"

"Yes, all right!" She put down her coffee mug a little too hard and took Christophe's hand in hers, holding it tightly. I saw her hand was shaking.

"It was an accident. You have to believe us."

"What was an accident?" Gabriel asked sharply.

"We just wanted to…" Sophie said, looking at me. "Look, I'd never seen the diamond and Grandfather guarded it so fiercely. We were curious, that's all. Then for my birthday, he gave me those little red earrings. Do you remember? I took them to a jeweler to be reset and he told me they were diamonds. Blood diamonds! I had no idea! I got to wondering if he'd had the stone cut up. If he had, then maybe he wouldn't miss a few diamonds. We could sell them, and then along with my earrings we could finally get the money for a place of our own."

Nic turned to Gabriel sharply. "Have you heard of this? Of blood diamonds coming on the market?"

"No, but if they were small ones, I probably wouldn't have."

Nic turned back to Sophie. "Go ahead. Tell us what happened that night."

"The night before it happened, you remember the bad storm we had? All the thunder and lightning? The power had gone off in the whole house and I heard Camille say she'd noticed a fuse had blown in the cellar when she went down to get a bottle of wine for dinner. I started thinking that maybe Grandfather hadn't replaced the fuse. I thought maybe the locks…"

"No, Sophie," Christophe said, "don't lie to them. It was me who asked about the locks. I told Sophie that maybe if the fuse still hadn't been replaced, we could go in and just take a few diamonds out of the vault."

"Okay," Gabriel said. "Then what? Once you had the stones, did Abel come down to the cellar?"

Sophie shook her head. "We never got that far. We went downstairs and right after we arrived, I heard Grandfather coming down behind us. It was so late, he should have been in bed asleep. But he came in and saw us and…oh, he was so angry. Furious. He knew what we had come for, like he always knew. He flew at us and called us both awful names and said we were ungrateful, and he was going to throw us out. We tried to leave."

"But he blocked our way," Christophe said. "Then he pulled back his hand to hit Sophie and I-I pushed him away from her."

"He fell and hit his head," Sophie said, tears streaming down her face. She reached for my hand. "But Beau, he was alive. I swear it! He was only knocked out. We panicked after I couldn't get him awake, though and we ran back upstairs. I was going to go to find some help, but…"

"But you didn't," Gabriel finished for her, his tone dry.

"No," she said, pulling away from my hand and covering her face. "We went back to our room and tried to decide what to do. And then after a while, I heard you calling us, Beau. And you said he was dead and the police were on the way."

"Did you take the blood diamonds?" Gabriel asked softly.

"No! I swear it wasn't us! I never even saw them! We had only just got to the cellar and opened the door when Grandfather came down the stairs."

"And tried to hit you?" Nic asked.

"Yes. I was mortified. He'd never raised a hand to me before."

"How long was it after you left the cellar before Rafe and Thibeau found him?"

"Maybe two hours. No more than that."

"Did you see anyone else in the cellar? Or on the stairs?"

"No," Christophe said firmly. "No one else was around."

"And do you remember seeing a book inside anywhere?"

"A book?" Sophie looked puzzled. "No, I never saw any books. He could have had them though. I remember seeing some shelves inside, and he always said he kept his important papers there."

"All right," Nic said after a moment. "I think we have what we need. You can go now."

Sophie looked at Christophe and then back at Nic. "But-but aren't we in trouble?"

"We may want to speak to you later. But for our purposes, we're satisfied, so you can go."

Sophie gave me an uncertain look, but got to her feet. Christophe stood up beside her and took her hand. He gazed down at me. "I'm sorry, Thibeau. I never meant to shove him so hard. I hope you believe me."

I nodded distractedly, still feeling shocked by their story. I could see it so clearly. Abel would have been beyond furious at what he'd have thought was a betrayal by the one grandchild he thought was most obedient.

"Do you—do you have to report this to the police?" Sophie asked, lifting her chin, her face still splotchy with tears.

I opened my mouth to reply and Nic spoke over me. "Of course."

She looked stricken but allowed Christophe to take her hand and lead her out of the room.

Gabriel got to his feet beside us. "Well, that's that. I have a meeting at twelve, so I need to get back to the hotel if you don't need me."

"No, go ahead. I'll catch up to you later." To me, he said, "Are you ready or do you need anything from your room?"

"Wait a minute, are you kidding me? You just sweep in here like-like Ghostbusters or whatever and take away the hex, like 'oh, just a death threat to Christophe, that's all.' And then you make my sister and her husband confess to-to assaulting Abel, maybe to *killing* him and my sister asks you if you're going to tell the police and you're like, 'of course,' and then Gabriel gets up like that's nothing and says, 'Have a meeting—gotta run.' Are you fucking kidding me?"

I stood glaring at him, my sides heaving with emotion after my tirade. He returned my glare with a cool regard.

"What do you want me to do, Beau? Wring my hands? Lie to the cops? As for the hex, I said I'd neutralize it. That's all I can do. We kept Christophe from seeing it, so hopefully, he'll be fine. I warned you earlier that we need to find this killer before he gets any stronger, but right now, he's still at large, still making threats and still extremely dangerous. All of us are at risk. As for what Sophie and Christophe did, I don't know what you want me to say. They didn't kill Abel, no. I believe Sophie's story. Whoever came in while he was unconscious and stabbed him ten times killed Abel. And we still don't know who that is. We have a little more information now, but still not enough to say definitively who did that. The only good news out of all of this is that Sophie or Christophe haven't been engaged in dark magic and that they didn't kill your grandfather. At least not directly."

"Oh, and the police are just going to take their word for that? You can see into her memories and you know she and Christophe didn't kill Abel. But *the police* can't! You're not telling the cops! I forbid it!"

"You forbid it? I told you that you couldn't interfere in our investigation. Was I not clear?"

"Oh, you were clear, all right. Now let me be clear. If you give Sophie and Christophe up to the police, you can forget about anything ever happening between us."

His face became cold and set. "Is that right?"

"Yes, it's right! If they were guilty, it would be one thing, but they didn't kill him, and there's no reason for their lives to be ruined by this."

"They may not have been the ones who stabbed him, but they left that old man for dead down in that cellar, make no mistake about that. They left him there bleeding and somebody else came along, maybe while he lay there helpless and killed him. I may not have liked him. Hell, I hate him for what he did to you, but what Sophie and Christophe did was wrong. Plain and simple. And you know it, too, or you would if you were thinking straight right now."

I turned away from him and crossed over to the window and kept my back to him. I was shaking with anger and hurt and the knowledge that he was right. That didn't make any of this any easier.

"How can I turn in my own sister?"

"You won't have to. Sophie will do it herself."

"What?"

After a moment Nic came up behind me. He didn't touch me but I could feel his warmth against my back. "I'm going to go now and talk to her and Christophe. It will be much better for them if they go to the police and tell them what happened. I'll contact my lawyers as soon as we get home and give them instructions. They'll take them down to the station in the morning and they'll be their attorneys of record. It's for the best, Beau. They can't move forward with this hanging over them." I felt a soft kiss on the back of my neck. "I'm sorry, *cher*. If I could change any of this for you, I would."

I sighed and turned to face him. "I know."

He held out a hand to me. "Let me take you to the car, and then I'll go speak to them. Try not to worry. Things will get better from here. Believe me."

Chapter Ten

Nic

I could tell Thibeau didn't believe a word I said about things being better once his sister Sophie and her husband turned themselves in for their part in Abel's death. And really, I hadn't been exactly truthful with him. I had no idea what would happen, and I was only trying to soothe him. I assumed that some of what the police might do would depend on the final autopsy report as to the actual cause of Abel's death—blunt force trauma to the head or the stab wounds. It would be helpful to know what kind of weapon was used too, but I didn't think the detective on the case would share that information readily. Not with me, anyway.

Time of death might factor into it too, since the old man might have lived if Sophie and Christophe had called for an ambulance right away. All of that would be in the autopsy report, which, as far as I knew, hadn't yet been released. Often the police held details like that back from the public until they caught the perpetrator. They also wouldn't look favorably on Sophie and Christophe not coming forward sooner to tell investigators what had happened.

I know what the *législateurs* would have done if we had been the only ones involved, which would have been to bind their powers for a time. Perhaps even confine them to one of the facilities we operated in a few out of the way parts of the world for practitioners who might abuse their powers if held in regular jails. It depended on how contrite we believed them to be and how willing they were to do better in the future. We'd take into consideration how young they both were as well. Poor judgement and youth often went hand in hand and trouble was a place you sometimes found yourself when you had a malfunction in judgment.

Not that I could convince Thibeau of any of that. He had always been extremely protective of his younger siblings and would expect me to intervene on his family's behalf. Which was not something I was able or willing to do.

He sat on the other side of the back seat, staring out the window all the way back to Dauphine Street, then slammed the car door a little too hard as he got out. I met Taylor's gaze in the rear-view mirror and sighed as he grinned at me. I knew Beau wasn't really angry at me so much as he was the situation. Still I felt like I was on the receiving end.

"I think I'll take off for a while, boss. Looks like you got some business to take care of."

"That I do. See you later, Taylor."

I got out of the car and went toward the front door, which stayed stubbornly locked, even with Beau making one pass after another over it. He turned to me, looking red faced and frustrated as I came up beside him. "You see? Not even a bit of magic left, like I told you. This is the easiest trick and one of the first ones I ever learned, yet *nothing*. It's all gone."

"I believed you, *cher*, and I know you don't have access to any of what's left in the ether. But I told you I'd fashion you a wand that would help, and I meant it. Come on, let's go out to the back yard and see what kind of wood is available. If nothing suits, I'll send Taylor to a park to look for something better."

I knew that his lack of magic wasn't really what was bothering him just then, but rather he was feeling powerless over the fate of his sister and her husband and his lack of magical power was just one more thing to frustrate him and become the focus of his anger. Like once when I got mad at one of my brothers, I yelled at my secretary. Then I had to spend the rest of the day abjectly apologizing and wound up giving her a raise and a dozen roses.

"What difference would a wand make anyway? I doubt that it will help."

"Oh, but that's where you're wrong. You must never have used one. Every wand is unique and they'll help you find your power and then direct it wherever you want it to go. It will depend for its character on the particular tree it comes from. And from its owner. Come on, let's go out here in the back. There are a few trees in the courtyard—let's see what we have to choose from."

We stepped out back onto the patio, and I looked around the small courtyard to see what the landscaper I'd hired during the renovations had done with the place. I had asked him for more mature trees when he did his work, but other than vaguely noticing the courtyard looked good, I hadn't paid it that much attention since I'd been back—way too much had been going on with Thibeau and his family. Now, though, I took the time to actually consider it.

While wands could be made out of most any wood, only a minority of trees could produce true wand quality wood—just as a minority of humans could produce magic. Each wood had different qualities and it was important to choose just the right one for Thibeau. Each wand, from the moment it found its ideal owner, would begin to both learn from and teach its human partner. I believed that Beau had enough magic left to draw on, with maybe a little boost from me, and though it might take years of practice, eventually he'd be brilliant at it again.

He was brilliant at most things, really, except submission. He wanted to submit and craved the domination I gave him, yet he fought it so hard. Every time. It was one reason we'd pulled back from it and even stopped altogether for a while before I got the news about going to New York. It was always something we talked about getting back into, but we'd thought we had our whole lives ahead of us.

Anyway, as I looked around the courtyard, I saw only two trees that might be suitable for our purposes. A good-sized dogwood tree and a young cypress.

Dogwood wands were quirky and mischievous. They had playful natures and insisted on having partners who could provide them with excitement and fun. It would be quite wrong, however, to think that dogwood wands weren't capable of serious magic. They've been known to perform outstanding magic, but an interesting little quirk they had was that they were sometimes a little loud when they worked, making an annoying tinkling sound, like little chimes when they cast a spell. I felt like a fairy godmother in a Disney film every time I used a dogwood wand. I still considered it though, until I saw an Inca dove perching in the lower branch of the cypress tree.

Inca doves were pretty little birds and considered lucky to find nesting in the leaves of any tree, because they never ever inhabited mundane, run-of-the-mill trees. They only liked trees that buzzed and hummed with power. I went over to the cypress and found a small branch lower down that looked suitable. I spoke to the tree softly, putting my hand on it and asking its permission to take one of its branches for Thibeau to use. It snapped off easily in my hand. Wands made of cypress found their match among the brave, the bold and the self-sacrificing. What better wand for someone like Thibeau Delessard?

I came back over to him. "I found the perfect branch. Now let's go inside and I'll show you how to use it."

We went back in, with Beau looking skeptical. "You just walked outside and snapped off a tree branch? That's it? And you expect me to think I can do magic with that thing. Are you going to try to use some kind of compulsion on my mind to trick me?"

"No, not at all." I finished snapping off all the little green shoots and extra bits and then held it out to him. "Take it."

He took it from me and jumped a little as the wand immediately got familiar with its new owner. "It's tingling."

"It's getting to know you, in a way. It has some power in it already and it recognized you. Now you have to try to find your magic and put it inside it."

"How do I do that? I told you it was gone."

"But it's not completely gone. Concentrate on remembering what it feels like to have power. Concentrate on the way it sings in your blood and your bones. Close your eyes and feel for what's left of your old power in the etheric flow. Here," I said, putting my hand over his. "I'll help you find it."

I closed my eyes, searching for my own magic, which leaped up to meet me like an old friend. Then I began to look for Thibeau's. I found it, huddled at the bottom of the flow, small and weak and a little ragged around the edges. Just like the little kitten that I liked to call him. My minou. I coaxed it out of hiding. I saw Beau smile as he felt it too, and I whispered, "Call to it. It's lost its way."

He closed his eyes and I felt him through our bond, reaching for his magic. It came to him and I directed it down into his hand and then into the wand. The wand lit up with a soft glow of inner fire for just a moment and then the glow gradually faded, leaving it looking like just an ordinary piece of wood. But we both knew it was so much more.

Thibeau gasped and looked over at me. "It's there. What's left of my magic is inside the wand."

"Yes, and you can use it whenever you need to. It's not strong yet, but I believe it will become stronger over time. The wand knows my touch now too, so whenever you need a little boost, it can find my power."

He turned shining eyes to me and smiled. "Thank you."

I lowered my head and claimed his mouth in a searing kiss. It was the most powerful kiss between us since we'd found each other again, even hotter than the one the other night when I realized how much I still loved him and how badly I'd been fooling myself that I was over him or could ever stay away from him once I'd found him again. I kissed him like I owned him—which in my mind, I did. He'd been mine since the first time I saw him in that bar.

I kissed him long and hard and then pushed him away, both of us looking at each other and panting for breath. I wanted him to be sure this wasn't just him being grateful. Thibeau closed his eyes for a long moment and then with a little sigh, he surged forward into my arms again. He cupped my face in his hands and held onto me, like he was afraid to let go. I returned the kiss with everything I had, putting all the passion I felt for him into it.

He was kissing me back sweetly, but almost chastely, his eyes and mouth closed, his full lips pressing into mine with excitement. I nudged those luscious lips open with my tongue and boldly swept inside, teasing his tongue with mine, then put a hand on the back of his neck and held him in place, moving my hand down to his groin and cupping him through his jeans. He sighed softly into my mouth, so I loosened his buttons and got inside his pants to stroke him. He let me have my way and it thrilled me.

When it finally became necessary for us both to breathe again, I pulled away and stared down into his eyes. His were still shining at me with excitement at the promise of the return of some of his power. I slid my lips over his again and again, the wet heat of them making my head spin. He relaxed in my arms, letting go and giving himself over to whatever was about to happen. It was rare for him to submit to me so completely and I planned to make full use of it. I picked him up and moved us both over to the sofa, where I began to undress him, pulling his clothes off and pushing down his underwear. I had to get my own clothes off too and I cursed the time it took to do it. I needed to have my hands on him again.

I put him on his back on the sofa and bent over him, licking the length of his cock with one long, slow swipe of my tongue. He cried out with pleasure. Closing his eyes, he moaned and let his head fall back. I leaned over and whispered in his ear. "I'm going to make love to you so hard and so slow right in this little ass. Just like that first time we made love. Do you remember? When I held you up against that wall and made you beg?" He looked up at me, still looking dazed, but he smiled, and his eyes were full of little sparks. He was breathing hard, his long eyelashes coyly brushing his cheeks as he stole little glances upward.

"I remember."

He sounded almost drunk—finding power can do that to a witch sometimes, especially since it had been so long for him without it. I peered down at him again to see if he was completely aware of what was going on. As I gazed down into his pretty, dark eyes, Beau reached for me and squeezed my cock.

"What are you waiting for? I need you."

His legs went up in the air and I just smiled down at him. He was topping from the bottom again, always trying to run things, but I didn't mind. Not this time anyway. I was enjoying him too much.

"We don't have any lube in here. And Taylor could walk back in any minute. Let's take this to the bedroom."

"No, I don't care," he said. "I want you *now*." He held out his arms impatiently. Still grinning, I lay down on top of him and kissed and licked and nibbled my way down to the hard cock leaking against his stomach, but I didn't try to enter him. Not without condoms or lubrication. By the time I reached the prize I was after, Thibeau was writhing under me and his breathing was coming faster and faster with the promise of the attention coming toward his dick. He shivered when I put my lips to the tip, then arched his back and cried out. I took the heavy length of him into my mouth and swallowed around it, listening with pleasure to him swearing softly above me. Beau's hands went into my hair, not trying to force me, but tugging gently, holding on against the onslaught of pleasure.

"Oh God, that feels so good," he groaned and flung an arm across his face, as if to hide from his own enjoyment of what I was doing to him. I murmured something and the vibration made him cry out and arch his back again. He gripped the cushions beneath him, holding on desperately as if trying not to come so quickly. I only intensified my efforts, taking him in deeper, my fingers working the base of his hard cock until he whimpered again. For me, a good blow job always started out fast and hot, and I knew from previous experience that Beau was extremely sensitive.

I wrapped my arms around his thighs and bent him in half, shoving his legs against his chest, my hands on the backs of his thighs, spreading him wide open. I bent to slide my tongue over his entrance and listened to him squeal.

"Please! Please!" he cried, and I smiled up at him.

"Please what?"

I pressed my tongue inside him again, flicking it over his sensitive entrance and held him down as he slowly came apart. I added a finger and his back bowed up off the sofa. "Oh my God! Please…"

"What do you want, baby? Tell me."

Breathless, Beau glanced down at me and then shut his eyes tightly again and groaned. "You just love to hear me beg."

"You do it so well," I replied. I gave him another long stripe down his crease again and again, holding him tight enough that he couldn't move away, no matter how he squirmed and cried out.

"Please, Nic."

"Please what?"

"I-I need you…"

"If we had some lube, I'd have already fucked you into this sofa, but I don't want to hurt you, and somebody didn't want to go to the bedroom. Maybe next time you'll listen to me."

He moaned and I laughed softly at him. "Wrap your hand around your cock while I lick this pretty hole. Go on…I like to watch you come apart."

"Nic, please," he screamed again as I gave him another sample of my tongue and grabbed one of his flailing hands to put it on his cock.

"Stroke yourself." I applied some pressure over his hand to show him how to do it, because rational thought was almost gone by now and he knew it. "Like this…that's right. Show me how you pleasure yourself. Come on, *cher*."

He threw his head back and began to stroke while I relentlessly licked and tongued his ass, trying to make him come. He was trembling with lust at this point, and finally, I heard him cry out, and he began to spurt long strings of cum all over his stomach and chest. "Oh fuck," Beau cried out again and then collapsed backward, totally spent. His eyelids fluttered and his breath was coming in gasps. I brushed his hand away and pumped him through his orgasm, wringing every last bit of pleasure from it.

Though I hadn't come myself, I was glad to give him some relief. I wrapped my arms around his waist, hooked my leg over one of his and just before sleep claimed me too, I pulled a comforter on the back of the couch over us in case Taylor came back in. Then I then fell asleep with Beau's warm breath gusting gently against my ear.

XXXX

Thibeau

We were eating breakfast the next morning when the phone rang. Nic looked down at it and handed it to me. "It's your brother Rafe's number again."

I put the phone to my ear and started to say said hello and then all I heard was screaming. I jumped to my feet in alarm and Nic came over to me in two quick strides.

"What is it? What's happened?" I shouted into the phone, and finally I heard Rafe's voice. He'd been talking all along but I hadn't been able to hear him over Sophie's screams.

"Beau? Can you hear me? Get here as fast as you can! Oh my God, Beau! Get us some help! Sophie's going crazy!"

I started shaking so badly I almost dropped the phone, but Nic took it out of my hand. "Talk to me, Rafe. This is Nic Gaudet. What's going on?"

I could hear him shouting even though Nic had the phone. "Christophe is-is dead. Oh my God, it's awful. You have to come. Now! Please!"

"We're on the way!" Nic said, and Taylor appeared on the stairs behind him. "Hurry and bring the car, Taylor!"

He helped me sit down, because my legs wouldn't hold me up. Christophe was dead? Had he really said that? Things began to move in slow motion after that. I know we went outside and stood impatiently on the sidewalk waiting for Taylor to bring the car around. Nic made me go back in and get my wand. "Just in case," he said. I ran in and grabbed it then jammed it down in my back pocket and hurried back outside.

I remember Nic being on the phone with Gabriel, and I heard him make arrangements to meet him at Ravenwood, but I was operating on automatic pilot by that time and barely knew what was going on. The ride to Ravenwood passed in a blur and then we were pulling through the gate. We'd made it in record time, but Gabriel still managed to make it there before us.

We all rushed up the steps and found Camille in the hallway, her face buried in her hands. She was wearing a turban on her head and had on makeup, which she rarely ever wore. She must have been on her way out to one of her church group meetings when the trouble started. She was also shaking so hard she could barely stand. Her son Emmanuel was beside her, his hand on her shoulder. He had a pair of big hedge clippers in his hand, and they were dripping blood onto the floor next to him. His face was shocked and angry as he looked at us. "I wanted to call the police, but Rafe said not to. He said to wait for you."

"Thanks, Emmanuel. We'll handle it. Take care of your mother until I can come back, okay?"

"I planned to," he replied, looking at me a little belligerently.

What the hell was with this attitude? He had always been around, as long as I could remember, just like his mother. He was already a grown man when I had come there as a child, and I figured he was close to fifty by now or maybe just his late forties. He hadn't shaved that morning, so his scruff showed gray against his dark skin. As long as I'd known him, he'd been surly and bad tempered. He did his job and Camille more than made up for his bad attitude, but I could still hear Sophie sobbing and screaming in the parlor and all I could think of was getting to her. I didn't have time for his drama just then.

Nic apparently did. He stopped short when he saw the hedge clippers. "Whose blood is that?"

"More like *what*. I killed that thing in the hallway," Emmanuel said, his dark eyes narrowing. "Before it killed Sophie or my mother. I heard their screaming all the way out in the yard. It was coming for both of them, and I'm not sorry I killed it neither."

"What are you *talking* about? What thing?"

He lifted the gory clippers and pointed with them farther down the hallway. "That thing. There."

"Shit!" Taylor said softly, and I heard Nic and Gabriel's quick intakes of breath.

It was so dark in the hallway that I hadn't noticed it before. But the thing lying there looked as if it had lumbered out of the front parlor and had been headed down the hallway toward the kitchen. It was as large as a man, but it wasn't recognizable as any creature I'd ever seen. It had a head like a monstrous dog, but with only one eye in the middle of its forehead and a long, misshapen snout. Its body was like an alligator's, only shaggy with dark fur and it had longer legs. Its mouth was open wide, showing sharp, saw-like teeth. A green, viscous substance was mixed in with the red blood that was pooling underneath it and the creature had several jagged wounds on its head where Emmanuel had stabbed it with his hedge clippers. But the most horrible thing—the thing that had me drawing in a shocked and horrified breath—was that it had ripped and torn rags of clothing hanging from its body. The shreds looked like a red flannel shirt and some jeans.

The thing lying in the hallway had once been wearing clothes.

I glanced over at Nic in horror and saw that he was badly shaken too. "What *is* that thing?" I asked softly.

Rafe came rushing out in the foyer, glancing down the hallway at the creature and shuddering. "Thank Christ you're here. It tried to kill Sophie and Camille while they were both in the kitchen after breakfast. If Sophie hadn't stopped it, I think they'd be dead by now."

"But what is it?" Gabriel asked him, taking a step toward it.

"We think it's Christophe." He pointed down at it. "It's wearing his shirt."

I reeled back in horror and disbelief. I heard the words but they weren't registering on me. *"What? What did you say?"*

Nic pushed in front of me and went over to kneel down beside the body. "What the fuck happened here? Who did this?"

"I did," Sophie said, swaying in the doorway, her face pale and staring. "It's all my fault." She took a step toward the body and started screaming again, a long hysterical wailing that made the hair stand up on the back of my neck. Nic took a quick step toward her and grasped her by her shoulders.

"Nunc vado ad somnum," he said and the wild screaming and crying stopped. She swayed a moment and then collapsed gracefully

in his arms. Rafe and I both reached for her and eased her to the floor. I held her in my arms and just rocked her like I had when she was a baby and I hadn't been much older.

Nic came over to kneel beside us. "Take her up to her room and stay with her while we get this sorted out."

I glanced up at him quickly. Was he sending me safely upstairs while he took care of things? I resented it even as I recognized I was the logical one to take care of Sophie right now. I swept her up in my arms and Rafe, who had rushed over to her too, helped me carry her into the parlor. The room was in shambles, chairs overturned and lamps on the floor. A bookcase lay toppled on its side near the door, and on the coffee table, its pages opened wide, was a large book. I had an awful feeling that if I closed the cover, I'd see that it was the *Bestiare* from my dream. But that was impossible. That had only been some kind of nightmare and this one was all too horribly real.

I stood there, feeling sick as I looked down at it. "Get Nic," I managed to say, taking Rafe's arm. "Tell him to hurry."

Chapter Eleven

Nic

Two hours after we arrived at Ravenwood, I finally had things under some semblance of control. Sophie had been carried up to her bedroom by Beau. I had put her to sleep with a calming spell and Beau was upstairs with her, in case she woke up. Rafe volunteered to stay with the *Bestiare*. To be honest, none of us really wanted to go and deal with the horror in the hallway.

I got Gabriel to bring me some salt from the kitchen to lay a ring around the book on the coffee table just in case. I cautioned Rafe not to touch it or even look at it until I got back. He nodded uneasily, and I wondered if it was wise to leave anyone alone with the book. But he said he'd prefer that to going back out there and dealing with what was left of Christophe, if that was truly who or what the body was.

It was hard to imagine that the creature was actually Christophe Decoudreau, the nice enough, if rather bland young man I had met the day before. But according to Rafe, Sophie had found a large, old book in the parlor the night before that she thought should have been put away in the library. No one claimed to know how it got there, but Christophe had offered to take it to the library for her after they ate breakfast. Nobody knew exactly what happened next, but as Sophie and Camille had been cleaning up the kitchen, they heard something large banging around in the parlor, and making strange, loud growling noises.

Sophie had gone to the door in a panic and had seen the creature lurching down the hall toward the kitchen. She'd panicked, as anyone would have and hurled a spell at it. The spell slowed it down, but it kept coming, according to Camille when Gabriel and I interviewed her. Her son Emmanuel stood over her the entire time, though Taylor had taken possession of the hedge clippers and had taken them away to be put in a plastic bag and examined later.

"Sophie used her magic," Camille told us. "She tried to stop it, but when she couldn't, Emmanuel stopped it for good."

Gabriel glanced over at me in concern that the woman would mention Sophie's magic so casually, but I only shrugged. Like Beau had said, she had lived and worked in a house full of witches for over fifty years. It was foolish to think she didn't know what was going on around her.

"Exactly what did Sophie do?" I asked Camille gently, though her nerves seemed to be in better shape than mine.

"She reared back, like she was taking aim, then threw some kinda white light at him. It looked like ball lightning, and it sounded like a firecracker when it hit. She kept on throwing those things at the monster, but they only slowed him down. It kept coming. I ran to the back door and started hollering for Emmanuel."

"You knew Emmanuel was close by?"

"Yes. He told me before I left the house that he'd be cutting hedges in the front yard all morning. He come running around the house when I yelled for him and had those big hedge clippers in his hand. I pointed at the hallway, and he ran in there."

I turned to Emmanuel. "Then what happened next?"

He narrowed his eyes at me. "I pushed Sophie outta the way and hit it with my clippers, that's what happened."

"Just like that?"

"Yeah. Why? What do you mean?"

"You weren't frightened of it?"

"I didn't have time to be. It looked like it was about to eat Sophie. Then I guess it woulda started in on the rest of us."

"Indeed. Well," I said briskly, though I was far from feeling anything close to that, "why don't you take your mother home so she can calm her nerves? Then if you can, come back over here and help us dispose of the uh…remains. And don't say anything about this to anyone. What happened here this morning is not to be repeated outside these grounds. Is that understood?"

"I understand all right," Camille said, giving me a narrow look. Emmanuel simply frowned at me before taking her arm and leading her out the back door.

Taylor had come back in and stood in the hallway, looking down at what was supposed to be the remains of Christophe Decoudreau. "What the hell are we going to do with this body, boss? It doesn't seem right just to drag it outside and burn it."

"No, but that's exactly what we have to do. We'll wrap it in some blankets and douse it in kerosene. Then set it on fire and let it burn down to ash."

"You'll have to help it along then," Taylor said. "No regular fire gets that hot. Even in a crematorium where the fire gets up to like two thousand degrees Fahrenheit, they still have to crush the bones afterward. And it's going to take a while to burn."

"Yes, Taylor, I'm aware. And we'll help it along, as you suggest. But I think we'll spare Sophie the grisly details, shall we? Maybe we should gather some ash afterward for her. In case…"

"In case what?" Gabriel asked. "That thing wasn't her husband. Not the husband she knew anyway. And she can't very well tell anybody Christophe is dead. Too many questions would be asked, and the police would damn sure never believe anything we could tell them. They might think we killed Christophe, because we can't very well produce a body. And I don't know how they'd explain that creature."

I blew out a long breath. "Okay. Obviously, you're right. We'll wait a couple of days, and then Thibeau and his sister can file a missing person report. I guess. I've never dealt with a situation quite like this before."

"Well, before we can burn it, we have to get it outside. It's going to take all three of us, I think."

"I'll go see if I can find some blankets to wrap it in. Gabriel, get some cleaning supplies to get up the blood."

It didn't take us too long in the end. I called Emmanuel to bring his truck around, and I found a big cotton chenille bedspread in the first bedroom I came to upstairs. I grabbed it to wrap the body in, along with some towels to clean up the blood. When I got back downstairs, Taylor was wrapping the bloody head in some plastic trash bags. We spread out the bedspread in the kitchen and pulled the body on top of it. Then I cleaned the hallway with bleach to get up all the blood. We wrapped it all up together. Each of us took a corner of it and pulled the surprisingly heavy body out in the back yard. Emmanuel brought around an old truck he used for hauling, and we took the body to the back side of the big back yard, near a swampy area that wasn't near any roads. We doused it in kerosene and Gabriel and I lit it on fire. Emmanuel said he burned leaves and grass out back on a regular basis, so no one should notice the smoke as being anything unusual.

A witch's fire flamed up quickly and burned white hot, so it wouldn't be all that long until the body was reduced to an unrecognizable heap of charred and brittle bones. We stood around silently while it burned, exhausted and sick. None of us knew what to say. Emmanuel got back in his truck without a word and drove back to the house.

Taylor volunteered to stay with the body until it completely burned, then crush the bones with his shovel, salt the ashes and bury what was left. Gabriel and I made our way back up to the house to check on the book we'd left with Rafe. I didn't like the idea of anyone being around it for long.

"Did Thibeau say this is the same book he dreamed about?" Gabriel asked. "Or did his dream bring it to reality?"

"It's the same, and I don't think his dream did it. Beau has lost most of his magic, like I explained to you earlier. He lost that two years ago."

Gabriel's face tightened at the reminder of our mother's part in it and he nodded.

"No," I said, "I think the dream was actually some kind of memory coming back. He used to spend time in his grandfather's library when he was growing up. That's where he found the Grimoire, the Rauskinna that Abel put away in his vault. Maybe he found this book too. I don't know. But the book is obviously very real."

"But how did that creature crawl out of the book? What made it a reality? Did somebody cast a spell to make it come alive? I can't do that. Can you do that?"

"No."

He shook his head. "The damn book needs to be destroyed."

Since I wholeheartedly agreed, we hurried back to the front parlor and found Rafe still nervously guarding it. "I'm glad you're back. I don't like being so close to this thing. It wanted me to look at it. I could feel it."

"That must have been how it caught Christophe."

I sent Gabriel upstairs to check on Thibeau and his sister, and I went over to the fireplace where Rafe had already laid a fire. When I glanced over at him, he shrugged. "I had to do something to keep busy and distracted while that damn book kept calling to me. I figured I'd better wait on you before we burned it."

I started the fire with a snap of my fingers and a muttered word. "*Ignis*." The white-hot flames leaped up, and I hurled the book inside the fireplace, ignoring the muffled cries that immediately started coming from the book. They actually sounded a little like animals. But if any creatures actually had been trapped in the Bestiary, then death would be a welcome release from the perversions the book had made of them. Personally, I thought the damn thing was a liar and trying one last ploy to avoid burning.

I turned back to Rafe. "Sit down, and let's have a conversation while we make sure it burns to ash."

He sat down across from me, looking wary and a little defiant. He'd never looked more like his brother to me. "Where were you last night?"

"How do you know I wasn't right here?"

"Because nobody mentioned you running in to help kill that thing, and I presume you would have heard all the screaming. No one sleeps that soundly."

He flushed. "Okay, I spent the night with a friend last night. I came home right after Emmanuel killed..." he rubbed his hand over his face. "God. I got home right after Emmanuel killed Christophe."

"What's the name of the friend you were with?"

"I'm not going to tell you that!"

I sighed. "You will, one way or the other. I have no interest in your love life, but someone has been casting spells against your brother, and now Christophe is missing, probably consumed by that book or turned into a monster. Your sister is in shock and I mean to have the truth of who has turned warlock in this house."

He jumped to his feet, and I put him forcibly back in the chair. He fell down unmoving and looked up at me wonderingly. "God, you're powerful! But whatever you're thinking about my family, you're just wrong. I have no idea who's doing this, but none of us has turned warlock!"

"Give me the name of who you spent the night with so we can check your alibi. Don't test me again, Rafe. Two men have already died."

"Don't you think I know that?" He fumed a little more and then huffed out a sigh. "Okay. I was with Gage Arceneau."

"The detective on your grandfather's case?"

"Yes," he replied, looking miserable. "We met before this ever started. Before Abel was murdered. He told me it was inappropriate and wants to break it off—at least until the investigation is over, but…"

"But you're hardheaded like your brother."

He glanced up at me sharply, unsure if he should resent that on his behalf or on his brother's.

"What time did you get home?"

"It must have been about nine-thirty this morning. I was coming up the front steps right after Christophe… anyway, I heard Sophie screaming."

"And then what?"

"Then I called you and Beau."

"All right. Go upstairs and sit with your sister. Beau is up there too." I listened for a moment to the screams I could still hear emanating from upstairs again. "Damn it. Work on a spell to keep her calm. She's making herself ill. And Rafe?" He looked back at me.

"Be careful. This is escalating. The warlock wants you all dead."

His eyes widened but he turned to go. I stayed by the fire to make sure every trace of the book was gone. Then I found a bag in the kitchen, scooped up all the ashes and put them in the bag. I was just finishing when Gabriel came into the parlor.

"I've burned the book. Now we need to salt these ashes and put them in an iron box before we bury them."

"Taylor and I can take care of that for you. I'll be glad of a chance to get out of this house for a while anyway. The atmosphere is horribly oppressive. Even worse than before."

"Yes, it's still being stripped. That last spell with the book took enormous power. Since Christophe is dead, and I think we've fairly well determined neither he nor Sophie was a warlock...?"

"Yes, I agree."

"Then that leaves Rafe and the servants."

"And Thibeau," Gabriel said.

"It's not Thibeau. I'd know if it was." He gave me some side eye and I shook my head. "Feel free to examine him if you have any doubts. But I'm telling you, you'd be wasting your time. I've searched through the etheric flow for his magic and what's left is not dark. There was only a little of it, actually, and I put it in a wand for him."

"All right, then, that leaves us three suspects, if you still believe it was someone in this house. Rafe, Emmanuel and Camille." He folded his arms and shook his head. "To tell you the truth, I don't think Rafe is involved. He's a stubborn ass, but I don't see feel any darkness in him."

"Neither do I. Did you notice the turban Camille was wearing by the way? And the makeup?"

"Yes. Concealing burns or redness, do you think?"

"Yes, I do," I said, nodding firmly. "If she's the warlock, her burns would have been by far the most severe and would have taken the longest to heal, even if she used healing spells. Hair doesn't grow back quickly, no matter how many magic spells you chant."

"You think Emmanuel is helping her?"

"Undoubtedly. He must have been the one to kidnap Thibeau and take him to that club. He may have had some unwitting accomplice. A friend or acquaintance who helped him get in unnoticed that night at the club, but I didn't feel anything dark inside the club as I entered that night. Nothing more than usual, anyway. I wonder if either he or Camille might have any kind of background in voodoo?"

"Hmm. Easy enough to find out. Let me make a few calls."

"I think that's a good idea. While you're at it, call your contacts down at Public Records to find out what you can about Abel Delessard. And about his will. We need to know why she's doing this, and why she wants the entire family eliminated. If she stands to inherit anything, motive might be important. First Abel, and Thibeau. And now Christophe."

"It's worth looking into."

"Good. See what you can find out. In the meantime, I'm going up to collect Beau and his family and take them back to Dauphine Street."

"I was wondering," Gabriel said, stopping me as I stood up. "The spell this morning—do you think it was intended to kill both Christophe *and* Sophie?"

"Maybe so."

"I'm not sure then why Emmanuel killed it before it killed her. Then they would both have been out of the way."

"Unless he didn't want her out of the way. He may have had designs on her himself after Christophe was gone. Or the situation wasn't as easy to control as they thought it would be."

We were both quiet for a few moments, thinking about it. Then Gabriel sighed. "I wonder if Christophe was still inside that thing and knew a little of what was happening to him. He could have gone after Emmanuel to protect Sophie."

We were both silent for a moment. "I guess we'll never know for sure," I said. "I *hope* he wasn't all that aware of what was happening to him." Gabriel looked back up at me. "That would have been beyond horrible."

"I know."

Gabriel sighed. "Well, what do we do now?"

"We go after them. The Rauskinna and the diamond must be in that house with them. But not now. Now we regroup and make plans."

"They have to know we're narrowing down the suspects."

"Probably. That's why we need to move as fast as we can on this. This house is too stripped to go up against Camille and Emmanuel here. It's better to take the fight to them at a place and time of our choosing. Find Taylor and get him up here. Let's meet at the front door in ten minutes."

XXXX

Thibeau

By the time Nic came upstairs, Sophie was in a deep sleep, helped along by Rafe's magic. Rafe was sprawled in a chair beside her, still suffering from the shock of what he'd seen downstairs, and both of us were worried sick about Sophie. She'd always been high-strung and excitable, and I didn't know what kind of damage the trauma of seeing her husband like that might have done to her. I was pacing restlessly at the foot of Sophie's bed when Nic came in.

He came directly over to me and caught me in a hard embrace. I put my head down on his shoulder and buried my face against his throat, just breathing him in. I just kept thinking how quickly we could lose the ones we loved the most in the world. We'd come close to losing each other once, but Christophe's death was permanent and forever. God, poor Christophe and poor Sophie. I honestly didn't know how or even if she would ever recover from this. I didn't think I'd have been able to.

After holding me close for a moment though, Nic eased me away from him. "We need to talk. Let's go out in the hallway. Rafe, you come too."

Rafe got to his feet and feeling puzzled, I followed Nic out to the hallway, leaving the door open so we could still see Sophie. Nic waited until we were both there and then glanced over his shoulder down the empty hallway. "We're going to my house in the city for the night. Please don't argue and don't stop to take anything with you. Believe me when I tell you this is a matter of life and death. I don't want you to stop long enough to even take anything. I can buy anything you need for tonight. Just bring Sophie and come downstairs. As quickly as you can."

"But I don't understand," I said, laying a hand on his arm. "What's going on?"

"*Cher*, please just trust me. We have to get you all out of this house. Now."

For once, Rafe didn't say a word, just turned around and went to gather Sophie in his arms. I glanced back at Nic, but took a blanket to wrap her in, and Nic led the way down the hallway and the front stairs. Gabriel and Taylor were waiting for us as we got to the door, looking relieved to see us. We all went outside and got in the cars. Sophie and I in Nic's back seat and Rafe in Gabriel's little convertible. We drove quickly through the gates without anyone

212

saying much. I could have sworn Taylor blew out a sigh of relief and glanced over at Nic in the front seat beside him as he did.

I leaned forward to speak to Nic. "Can you please tell me now what this is all about?"

He glanced back at me. "We think we know who the murderers are."

"Who?"

"You're not going to like it."

"Probably not, but tell me anyway."

"Camille and her son Emmanuel."

There was a brief silence and then I snorted in disbelief. "What? Seriously? Oh, please, Nic, that's insane."

"You called me Sherlock once. So, here's a quote for you directly from Arthur Conan Doyle's books. 'Once you eliminate the impossible, whatever remains, no matter how improbable, must be the truth.'"

"I told you that neither of them have a scrap of magic."

"I think that's all changed now."

"But why would they do such a thing? It makes no sense to me. Camille has been practically a member of the family for as long as I remember. And Emmanuel may not be the most pleasant guy to be around, but I always thought he was loyal."

"Nevertheless, Beau, I believe they killed Abel after Sophie and Christophe left him in the cellar, though I don't yet have a motive for it. They did have the means and opportunity, just like everyone else in the family, however. Now if we can find out why, we'll know for sure who the killers are." He glanced back at me and Sophie. "For both Abel and for Christophe," he added softly.

The rest of the trip to Dauphine Street passed in something of a blur. I was still reeling from Nic's theory and I was getting increasingly worried about Sophie. She was waking up some and once she opened her eyes and stared at me with absolutely no recognition on her face. I told Nic and he'd promised to send for a doctor as soon as we got her to his home.

Once we arrived, we carried her, completely unresisting, into the house and I put her down on the bed in Nic's room, and made sure she was as comfortable as I could make her. When I came out, everyone was standing tensely around the living room and Nic said he had a doctor on the way.

"A doctor is coming here?"

"Yes, a psychiatrist we've had dealings with before. He's very good and a practitioner. I told him he might need to treat her for shock. Don't worry, he's also discreet."

"And expensive, no doubt. Maybe we should take her to the ER."

"Don't worry about the money." He held up a hand to stop me from snapping at him. "And before you start, this is not about the money anyway. This is practitioner business and more specifically a *législateur* concern. Sophie's bills will be paid by us until further notice. We have to make sure she doesn't unwittingly expose our magic."

"If you two are through bickering, maybe you'd like to hear what I've been able to find out so far about Camille Dubois and her son," Gabriel said.

Nic gave his brother an irritated look, but turned toward him impatiently. "Well, then?"

"According to my contacts, there is no record of any marriage for 'Mrs.' Dubois. Her son Emmanuel's, birth certificate has the father listed as John Smith. His race is listed as White and his age as thirty-nine. No address listed. Camille was twenty-four. Her address was Ravenwood."

"Yeah, that's probably about right. She's been there a long time."

Nic nodded thoughtfully. "And the ages match."

"Match what?"

"That would make Camille seventy-two now, which is about right. And it would have made the father eighty-eight. Which I believe was Abel Delessard's age at the time of his death."

My mouth fell open. Rafe, who had apparently already heard this information on the way here in Gabriel's car, didn't seem as shocked.

"What are you saying? Camille and Abel!"

"Why is that so shocking?" Nic asked. "She was no doubt a pretty woman forty-eight years ago, and your grandmother would have been dead by then for several years. She was living there on the estate and in the same house. Your father had recently married and left home to raise his family."

"But why would he never have told us? And why did he never claim Emmanuel as his son?"

"You'd have to ask him," Gabriel said, "but I can think of a few reasons. Camille was much younger and a different race. To a man like Abel Delessard, that would have mattered."

"But that's awful! Wait a minute, you mean he made her and their son move out of the house when we came there to live?"

Rafe made an odd sound. "God, no wonder Emmanuel always acted like he hated us. How old would he have been when we came there to live?"

"About twenty years old."

"And Abel made him move out to the groundskeeper's house, along with his mother, while we came in and probably one of us took his room. You're right—no wonder he hated us."

"Wait a minute," I said, still trying to wrap my mind around it. "None of this means that Camille and Emmanuel killed Abel. If they were going to do that, the time would have been when he denied them both and moved them out to that old shack out back."

"Not necessarily," Gabriel said. "Maybe he made her promises to get her to keep quiet about their relationship all those years. He may have told her he'd left her and her son something in the will."

"But I knew Grandfather left everything to Nic. He's the oldest grandson and so he would inherit everything. That's just the way our family has always been."

"Maybe Camille didn't know that," Nic said. "Is there any way she might have recently discovered that information."

Rafe snorted. "The epic fight that Beau and Abel had the night he got killed. At dinner."

Nic looked at me incredulously. "They mentioned that at the dining room table? With Camille in the next room? Might she have heard them?"

"The fucking neighbors probably heard them, and the closest ones are three miles away. And they didn't just mention it—they were screaming at each other. Abel said he'd left everything to Thibeau and talked about how ungrateful he was for that. And Beau said he didn't give a damn about the estate and to give it away, because it had already cost him everything. Yeah, I meant to ask you what you meant by that, bro. Anyway, she sure as shit heard the whole thing. We all were shocked by how heated it got."

Nic looked over at me and his eyes were stormy and sad on my behalf. I lifted one shoulder in a shrug. "If I'd known about Camille and Emmanuel, I would have taken care of her once the estate was mine. I always planned to share with the rest of the family, and I never would have cut them out."

"Some people don't like to share," Nic said.

Taylor spoke up then too. "She might have felt like you had no right to the estate anyway. Her son was next in line. He was Abel's son."

"That's true. I wish she had come to me and told me how she felt. She *was* wronged, but to take it out that way on Abel and on poor Christophe…" I choked up then and had to turn away. Nic came to stand beside me. "Don't forget what they tried to do to you. She was gravely wronged, yes. But she did far greater wrong by her actions. She and her son will both face judgment now." He turned and looked at each of us in turn. "The book and the blood diamond have given her and her son power. It's up to us now to take that power away. And I think it's going to take our combined strength to do it."

XXXX

Nic

The doctor arrived on schedule and spent a long time in Sophie's room with her. He called both her brothers in at one point for a long discussion, along with some raised voices, but when they finally emerged, both brothers looked shocked and saddened.

Beau came directly to me and rested his head against my chest. "He said she has acute stress reaction, and doesn't think she'll come out of it on her own. She's already showing signs of dissociative symptoms, and it may develop into PTSD or even dissociative amnesia. She didn't seem to know either Rafe or me. The doctor would like to take her to his private clinic for a while to treat her. He said he can treat her with drugs, counseling and psychotherapy after a few days. Then when she's calmer, he can tell us more."

"What do *you* think about that plan? I know that hospitalization is a sensitive subject for you."

"It is, but I want what's best for her. Rafe agrees. And she's not going to be committed. I'd never do that to her. She agreed to go, though I don't think she actually knows what's going on. I just want them to see if they can help her."

"When would he take her?"

"Tonight." He raised his eyes to the ceiling like he was trying to keep tears from falling and took a deep breath. "She needs help, Nic. Rafe and I said okay." He looked at me then, his eyes wary. "What about what she and Christophe did the night Abel died? Will you still have to go to the police?"

I shook my head. "Christophe is dead and she's suffering. I don't wish to add to it. Let's leave it at that for now."

He nodded and closed his eyes in relief. I held him close for a few minutes, while the doctor made some calls. Not long after, two young nurses arrived and they took Sophie out with them. The doctor's clinic was in town and very highly respected. I explained all this to Thibeau and Rafe as they sat on the sofa, looking like somebody had kicked them. When Sophie passed by us, she was awake, but looked dazed and confused. She never even glanced at any of us.

"You can go see her tomorrow," I said, trying to soothe him.

Beau nodded, and I hugged him to my side, feeling fiercely protective. We had to figure out how to stop Camille and her son and then nothing would ever hurt him again if I had my way.

Gabriel, who had been holding the door and helping get Sophie to the doctor's car, came back in and sat down across from us. "I have some more news about Camille. The voodoo priest I know over in

Jefferson Parrish got back to me. Camille belongs to a group that practices only the darker aspects of voodoo."

"What's the difference?" Rafe asked.

"Voodoo is actually closer to being a religion. In voodoo there's a visible and an invisible world, and these worlds intertwine. Death is only a transition to the invisible world. An important part of voodoo is the Lwa, or 'the invisibles.' Unlike saints or angels, the Lwa were not simply prayed to, they're served. In rituals, the Lwa, like Baron Samedi, are called on by the priests and the witches, to take part in the service, receive offerings, and grant requests. The *législateurs* deal with practitioners of dark magic, whatever they called themselves. Camille may have a church she attends—the Methodist Episcopal church you mentioned to Nic. But she also practices voodoo. Like all magic, whether it's light or dark depends entirely on the *intentions* of the practitioner. And I think it's safe to say that Camille's intentions, from what we know at this point at least, are dark."

"I'd say you're right," I replied.

"What we've seen so far has definitely been voodoo. Some of the most important spirits in voodoo are the dead, the predecessors to the invisible world…particularly the recently dead. Some voodoo practitioners try to contact these spirits of the dead for advice and guidance, or to ask questions. Some, like Camille, contact them to make them do their bidding."

"How the hell do they do that?"

"Through necromancy. By calling the dead."

"Well, that sounds pretty damn grisly," Taylor said. "Just like everything else about this case has been."

"Taylor," I said warningly.

"No, he's right," Rafe said with a shake of his head. "Just when I don't think things could get a whole lot worse, it does."

"I'm afraid it's not done yet." Gabriel replied. "There's more."

"God, what *else*?" Beau asked.

"Your grandfather was broke. Like in serious financial condition. That check you wrote to pay for his funeral, Beau? It's going to bounce, if it hasn't already."

Thibeau put a hand to his forehead and groaned. I felt for him. He'd experienced one disaster after another and Gabriel said it wasn't done yet. "Abel Delessard has been selling off small diamonds of two or three carats for the past three years now. And not just any diamonds, but diamonds with a distinct brownish red hue."

"Blood diamonds."

"You got it. And here in New Orleans, right under our damn noses. He kept them small, no doubt for that very reason, and dealt with a private broker, so no one would ask too many questions."

"That old son-of-a-bitch was selling off pieces of the cursed De Lys Diamond!" I said.

"Yes, he was. We don't know for how long. Which means he may or may not have had that many pieces of it left. One reason he never showed the diamond to anyone and kept it hidden in that vault."

"I wonder if Camille knew about it?" I asked.

"I don't know. She has to have found some of the diamonds though, because they've been fueling her power."

"She must have all of them that were left," Rafe said softly.

"Maybe so. But she might think he had more of them that he's hidden somewhere in the house. I have a theory too about why Emmanuel might have stabbed Christophe with those hedge clippers. If they'd managed to kill Thibeau and Rafe, along with Christophe, Camille might have talked Sophie into marrying Emmanuel, which would have given them the estate."

"But from what you've told us, Emmanuel is Sophie's uncle!" Taylor protested.

"Half-uncle and so what?" I said. "Someone who commits murder would probably barely flinch at incest."

Beau gave me a look and I shrugged. "Just saying."

"That's disgusting."

"So is murder, *cher.*"

"So what's the plan?" Rafe asked. "Do we go to the estate and arrest her and Emmanuel?"

"No, we can't," Gabriel replied. "Because they left."

"What?"

"I called the police station and talked to Detective Gage Arceneau. I told him what we knew about Camille and her son. The parts pertinent to his case, that is. He decided he'd like to have a word with them, too, but when the police arrived, Camille and Emmanuel had cleared out everything from their house and they were gone. The police are looking for them."

He looked over at me. "And I presume we are too."

"Damn right. We need to scry for a location."

Less than an hour later, we had everything set up. Gabriel was better at scrying than I was, maybe because I couldn't focus for such a long time. Scrying wasn't a way to see the future, no matter what some people said about it. The future can't be seen, it can only be speculated about, based on present information. It was more of a way to find out present information, some of which a person might already know or be aware of on a subconscious level. It's also a way to tap into second sight to reveal the unseen. Gabriel helped his along with a generous push of his magic.

Scrying was simple enough to do. Gabriel required only a wooden bowl, a crystal and some candles, all of which I had readily available. He put some water in the bowl, set the crystal inside next to the candles and got the room nice and dark. Then I handed him a small knife and he cut his little finger and let the blood drop into the water.

Once the spell was cast, he gazed into the light reflected by the candle into the water and waited for the images to come to him. Usually, it didn't take him too long to fall into a bit of a trance-like state and relay the images he was seeing in his mind.

The room was full of people tonight and that didn't help, though everyone tried hard to keep quiet and stay still. After a few minutes, Gabriel began to chant a little spell to himself, over and over. It wasn't what he was saying so much as the cadence of it. It helped him to achieve the trance.

HEXXED

He looked up at me and his eyes had absolutely no color in them. He began to speak, so softly I had to strain to hear him. "Witching hour. Wind and rain. Touch the corpse again and again…three times needed to make the charm. Berald, Lazarus, Herod, Garm…"

His eyes flew open and he was himself again. I took his cold hand in mine to bring him all the way back. "Good, Gabriel. You did it. Now tell me what you saw."

He took a few gasping breaths and Taylor passed him a bottle of water. He turned it up and drank almost half of it before he could speak to us.

"They plan to raise the dead at the cemetery where Abel was interred. Camille and the others. They're going to Abel's grave, because he's newly dead and they think they can make him tell them where the diamonds are hidden. They won't let him rest until he does."

"Good God," I said softly, and I heard Thibeau gasp behind me. I turned around and took him in my arms.

"We'll stop them, *cher*. These *putains*. I promise you."

"I know," he said, shaking his head. "And I'm ready to help you. I need to go with you, Nic. Don't leave me behind."

"I'm through leaving you behind. You're with me tonight. And it may just take all of us to end this thing once and for all."

XXXX

Thibeau

224

HEXXED

A graveyard at midnight in the company of witches was not anywhere I thought I'd be when I woke up that morning. Yet here I was, going back to the cemetery where my grandfather had been buried only a few days before.

Abel had been buried in St. Louis Cemetery No. 1., a cemetery that was famous in New Orleans, and which was featured on the National Historical Register. It was also the place where the famed voodoo priestess Marie Laveau has her tomb. It's a Catholic cemetery, though it has a Protestant section generally not vaulted, in the northwest section of the huge cemetery, and Abel was nominally Protestant, or so he said.

He really wasn't anything I could tell, though he shared a lot of Fundamentalist beliefs. However, our family, the Delessards, had owned a crypt in the cemetery for many, many years, so that's where Abel was entombed. Right there in the middle of the Catholics. It was the cheapest option and considering what I'd learned lately about our finances, probably the best I could have done for him anyway.

In this "city of the dead," elaborate, crumbling above-ground vaults and crypts hinted at the stories of the long dead men and women entombed there. It was a chilling place to be in the hour after midnight.

The best time for necromancy was, as might be expected, from midnight to one in the morning. The old people said that the hour after midnight was the most evil hour. If a bright full moon hung in the sky when one went to raise the dead, that was fine. But even better was a storm-tossed night, one filled with wind and rain, thunder and lightning. And it wasn't just for effect. Spirits, or so the old people said, had trouble showing themselves at any other time.

Unfortunately, or fortunately to my mind, it wasn't storming, so at least we wouldn't have to endure the rain, but the night was dark, with only a crescent moon in the cloudy sky, just like in all the horror movies. We arrived just before eleven, wearing dark clothing and ready to end this thing once and for all. I stayed close to Nic and I clutched the wand he made me. It hummed to itself 0as we walked down the seemingly endless rows of tombs and crypts.

Once located at the marshy city limits, St. Louis Cemetery is now near the center of the city, thanks to the draining of the swamps, so we didn't have far to drive that evening. We parked in the shadows of a side street and made our way through the gloom of night to the cemetery. I couldn't help holding tightly to Nic's hand in superstitious dread of what the night would bring, and I didn't dare look left or right for fear of seeing a spectral face peering through the bars of one of the crypts. Some people said vampires roamed the cemetery at night, but I didn't think there was much danger of that. They did exist, but they were after the living, not the dead.

One of the first things you saw when you enter St. Louis Cemetery No. 1 was a bank of "wall vaults" to the left. These tombs had coffins stacked on top of each other, filing cabinet style. Some were only partially visible—the rest were below the earth, evidence that New Orleans was gradually sinking. Our family vault was a wall vault, near the center of the cemetery, and it housed the remains of countless Delessard family members. I knew where the tomb was, since we'd been there only days before at the interment, but I had forgotten a lot of cemetery lore. I heard Rafe speaking softly to Taylor as we walked through the rows of vaults.

"After a body is interred," he whispered, "the family leaves it undisturbed for a year and a day. At that point, the remains can be pushed to the back of the vault, leaving room for another body. But once it's filled, like ours is, the family has to collect the remains and put them in muslin bags, to be stored at the back of the crypt."

"I thought that caused their ghosts to walk," Taylor replied in a hoarse whisper. "That's what they say in the TV shows anyway. That messing around with graves and disturbing a body's rest can disturb the spirits."

I heard Rafe chuckle. "I guess that's why this cemetery is so haunted."

I shuddered and Nic said, "Cut it out, you two. We don't know what time they're coming. Be quiet as you can once we get close. I don't want to scare them off."

Personally, I didn't think much would scare Camille or Emmanuel, as they'd already proven, but everybody quieted down just the same, and we settled down to wait.

When we arrived at the Delessard vault, we spread out, hiding behind nearby wall vaults. I was still holding tightly to my wand and staying plastered up against Nic as we stood on the left side of the vault beside the Delessard crypt. Rafe was opposite us behind another crypt and ducked down out of sight. Gabriel and Taylor were on the far right of ours. I couldn't see them in the dark shadows, but I knew they were there. I hated everything about what we were doing, but I had to be present to confront Camille. Nic had told us before we arrived that we were to keep quiet until she worked her spell to raise the dead, because he wanted there to be no question of guilt. She and Emmanuel had earned themselves a death sentence for their actions, and Nic and Gabriel would execute it tonight.

Assuming we managed to defeat them, that is, which to my mind was not at all a sure thing. I knew how powerful Nic was, but that night the fire came into our room, the evil had been palpable and real. Surely Camille's powers had only grown since then.

Or had they? Was that why she was here tonight seeking more? She had no power of her own to regenerate, so was she slowly but inexorably stripping the diamonds the way she'd stripped the house? We'd soon find out. I shivered and drew closer still to Nic's back.

He turned to look down at me. "Cold, *cher*?"

I was, a little. Because of the night's chill that came off the lake once the sun had gone down or just the atmosphere of the cemetery, I wasn't sure why, but I did feel a distinct coldness. We'd been waiting for a while by that time and I craved Nic's warmth and light. He wrapped an arm around me and pulled me even closer.

"You know," I said softly, my voice barely above a whisper. "I haven't slept with anyone else in all the time we were apart. At first, I was too hurt and too ashamed, and then I just never found anyone who made me feel the way you did."

He leaned down and brushed his lips across mine. "No matter what happens," I whispered to him. "I love you."

He pulled up my chin and gazed into my eyes. "Nothing will happen. You stay behind me, and don't argue with me, please. The wand is new and you're not used to it yet. Just-just be cautious, okay?"

I pulled Nic's head to mine and kissed him hard. "Beau," he whispered and lifted me off my feet, pinning me against the wall. It didn't seem to matter to either of us how inappropriate this was, with my brother nearby and his too. Waiting for people to come and raise the dead. I wrapped my legs around him, driving my mouth against his and rutted against his hips shamelessly.

"I want you so much. Please, Nic."

"Even if I could get past the idea of making love in a cemetery, surrounded by hundreds of corpses, I don't have any condoms with me, *cher*."

I laughed softly in his ear. "I don't think they'd mind. And like I said, I haven't been with anyone else."

"I have," he said, blushing a little. "A few. But I get checked regularly. I'm healthy, I promise."

"Well, then?"

He groaned as I threw my arms around him again and tried even more persuasion. The passion between us, always simmering, blazed up, and it only took a few seconds to pull our clothing out of the way. He spun me around, pushed me so I was bent face first against the wall of the vault. No sweet words or preparation. He spit in his hand and slicked himself up, took hold of my hips and thrust into me. It was painful and rough, and I had to clamp a hand over my mouth to keep quiet. But I wanted it and I wanted him. Blood pounded in my cock painfully as he fumbled for it in the dark. He pulled his hand over it once, twice and then I was coming in his hand, biting down on my finger to keep from screaming his name. He fucked me through it and then he was coming too, filling me with his hot cum until it ran down my legs. Afterward, he clung to me as we both tried to recover. The passion had swept over us like a wave and then flung us up on shore, exhilarated and gasping for breath.

I was almost surprised when we heard the sounds of low chanting coming toward us. Nic hurriedly pulled away from me, straightening his clothes, and I pulled my pants back up over the stickiness on my thighs. I leaned out, peering around Nic's broad shoulder to get a look at what was coming.

A group of dark figures were walking slowly toward us, carrying small torches. The figure in front came out of the misty fog that had begun to creep over the cemetery and resolved itself into Camille, carrying a bag, a candle and a large, thick book. She was wearing a long, dark dress, and a turban wrapped around her head. Three other women were behind her with Emmanuel bringing up the rear. I recognized the women as ladies from Camille's church, or so she had said when she introduced them to me. They had been among the ones who had brought the food to our home after Abel's death. It was hard to reconcile those motherly and grandmotherly figures with the women that came toward me now. Their faces were ghostly in the light from the torches they carried and set in grim lines. They each carried other objects their hands as they made their way toward Abel's apparently not-so-final resting place.

Camille placed some objects, including the book, on the ground in front of the crypt, then stood back from her accomplices. By the light of their torches, they drew a circle in the earth in front of the tomb they were planning to disturb. Emmanuel, the largest of the dark-clothed figures, dropped something in the disturbed earth, moving slowly but surely all around it. Then with a flick of a match, he set fire to the ring, which burned with a low, sullen blue flame.

Emmanuel rose and took a crowbar to the gate over the crypt, then disappeared inside. We could hear more loud, cracking noises coming from inside and it sounded as if he were breaking into the sealed coffin. A few minutes later, he confirmed the idea by emerging from the vault, carrying my grandfather's body. It was dressed in the white shirt and gray suit Sophie had picked out for him to wear, but I couldn't bring myself to look at his face.

Emmanuel laid the body inside the circle they had drawn, with its head to the east and its arms and legs arranged as if it were on the cross, a hideous parody of the crucified Jesus. Next to the body's right hand, Camille placed a bowl, then reached in her bag and pulled out a small bottle of wine and another of what looked like sweet oil. She poured from each bottle into the bowl and then pulled a wand from the bag. Camille picked up the book she'd been carrying, which had to be the Rauskinna, and opened it up. She began to recite a conjuration, touching the corpse with her wand three times.

I was feeling shocked and sick by this time, but I heard her words clearly. "By the Virtue of the Holy Resurrection and the agonies of the damned, I conjure and command thee, spirit of Abel Delessard, to answer my demands and obey these sacred ceremonies, on pain of everlasting torment. Berald, Beroald, Balbin, Gab, Gabor, Agaba, arise, arise, arise, I charge and command thee."

A hush fell over the entire cemetery, as if every living thing inside it were holding its breath. Then slowly, slowly, Abel's limbs began to twitch. He began to stand up!

A hoarse shout rent the air, ringing out across from us and suddenly Rafe leaped out of hiding.

"Stop!" he cried out, his voice shaking. "Stop this now, Camille! This is unspeakable! How fucking *dare* you desecrate my family's crypt and my grandfather's body this way?" He was sobbing as he hurled a ball of white fire at her with such force that when it struck her, it knocked her off her feet. He ran toward her, and I was right behind him, throwing off Nic's hands and hearing his and the others' hoarse shouts in my ears.

Rafe had leaped on top of her, but I went for Emmanuel, and even though he was much more powerfully built than me, I had surprise and sheer rage on my side in the fight. I struck him hard and we fell to the ground. I was vaguely aware that the women who had been with them were screaming their fright and running away down the corridor between the vaults.

232

Emmanuel, who had recovered from his initial shock, drew back his fist to slam it into my head. One of the blows fell on the side of my face and stunned me. I fell off beside him on the ground, and he rolled over to hit me again. Before he could land the blow, however, his fist was caught and held in Nic's hand, and he was wrenched up and away from me with such force that his body actually flew through the air and struck the vault on the other side of us with a meaty thump.

I heard Camille still screeching her rage and turned to see both Rafe and Gabriel grappling with her, but she was down and on her back. The Grimoire was lying beside her, so I grabbed it and threw it down on top of Abel within the ring of fire that surrounded him.

I pointed my wand toward it and repeated some of the words I'd heard Nic say in his spells. *"Defendat nos a malo! Ignis!"* I cried again and again, and a bolt of fire leaped from the tip of my wand directly down onto the center of the book. The dry pages of the ancient book caught up immediately and blazed high with a fire so hot I had to reel back away from it. I stumbled and fell sideways, landing on one knee. The flames licked out at me hungrily, before I felt strong arms pulling me away from it.

It was Taylor, who bent solicitously over me, shielding me from the worst of the heat for a moment with his own body. "Are you all right?" he yelled down at me and I nodded breathlessly. He picked me up and surged backward then, pulling me with him. Well on our backs on the path between the vaults.

233

The flames were already consuming Abel's body. Nic rushed over to us and pulled me to my feet as Taylor scrambled up to his. "Let's get out of here," he cried and we ran toward the north exit, with Rafe and Gabriel right behind us. I looked over my shoulder and saw Emmanuel's body lying lifeless, draped over the vault beside the Delessard's, his back bent over the roof at an unnatural angle. On the path lay Camille, her face upturned to the sky, her eyes wide and staring.

We could hear the sirens getting closer as we ran away, and I wasn't tempted in the least to turn and look back.

Epilogue

Nic

We managed to get back home and get cleaned up before the police came knocking on my door just before dawn. Gabriel and Taylor had left by then, Taylor going back to the hotel with Gabriel to spend the night, as Rafe would be sleeping upstairs in the loft.

We had the lights off, just lying in bed as we waited for the police to show up. When they did, we got up and let them in. We denied all knowledge of everything, of course. Gage Arceneau gazed at Rafe a long time after we'd told him we hadn't been out of the house on Dauphine Street since early that evening, and then he closed his notebook with a snap and put it away.

"The bodies of your elderly housekeeper and her son were found by the tomb of your grandfather, which had been broken into. His coffin had been destroyed and his body desecrated. His charred corpse was found lying in the middle of St. Louis Cemetery. Camille Dubois' neck was broken, and I believe the coroner will confirm her son died from blunt force trauma, when his body was picked up and *thrown on top* of a vault nearby." He looked at each of us in turn. "But you want to tell me you know nothing about any of this?"

"That's right, officer."

"Uh huh. And what about your sister and her husband? Where are they? We sent a patrol car to Ravenwood and found no one home."

"Unfortunately, we don't know where Christophe Decoudreau is at the present time. He and his wife Sophie had a terrible argument and he left, saying he wasn't coming back. Sophie got terribly upset, of course, so we brought her here and called in a doctor for her. She's at his private clinic now."

"I see. You say they had an argument."

"Yes."

"And he left. Which caused his wife to be so upset she had to be hospitalized."

I shrugged. "She's high strung."

"Uh huh. And this doctor will verify all that, will he?"

"He'll most certainly verify that he came here to examine her and that she's now at his clinic, suffering from acute stress, yes."

"And you don't know where her husband is?"

"No, sadly, we don't."

He got to his feet and glared at me. "I don't believe a fucking word of this, you know."

I took a step toward him, but Rafe stepped up between us, giving me a look that dared me to touch the detective. "I'm sorry, Detective Arceneau," Rafe said, giving me an irritated glare. "There's nothing more we can tell you. Order has been restored, now, and everything that you said that happened at the cemetery tonight was orchestrated by Camille Dubois and her son Emmanuel. I promise you that my sister is in good hands now, and my brother and I would never do anything to hurt her or her husband, Christophe. The same goes for the Gaudet family. None of this is due to anything we did wrong. I swear it."

The detective glanced uneasily between Rafe and the rest of us. I could tell he was torn, but he had nothing on us but deep suspicion. And even that had been somewhat assuaged by what Rafe had told him.

"You should investigate Camille Dubois and her son," I spoke up. "I assure you that none of us did anything wrong."

He looked at me another moment and then gave a little snort. "Well, since you *assure me,* Mr. Gaudet. I guess I can go home now." He gave us all another stern look. "I wouldn't advise any of you to leave New Orleans in the near future without letting me know. That goes for your brother and your driver too. Is that clear?"

"Yes, Detective. It's quite clear. I do have a business to run in New York, however, so I'd appreciate it if you'd let me know when Mr. Delessard and I would be clear to travel there."

"Which Mr. Delessard?" he asked sharply, and I smiled.

"Mr. Thibeau Delessard."

"Oh." He glanced over at Rafe. "I'll let you know," he said, and turned to leave.

"I'll walk you out." Rafe hurried after him.

"God," Beau said, sinking to the sofa behind him. "He didn't believe a word of that, did he?"

"No, I'm afraid not. He's bright and a good cop. Rafe seems taken with him."

"Yes, he does." Thibeau fell back against the cushions and sighed. "Oh, hell, we're going to be arrested, aren't we?"

I laughed and sat down beside him. "No, not at all. They can have all the suspicion in the world, but they have no proof of any wrongdoing on our part. What we did about Camille Dubois and her son was perfectly legal and the right thing to do, according to *our* laws."

"Yes, but what about Sophie? She's kind of a wild card. If she talks to the police…"

"It will be a while before she's able to speak to them. Then it might be necessary for Sophie to disappear for a while. No, don't look at me like that. Surely, you know I mean her no harm. There are clinics in Switzerland run by doctors who are also practitioners. We'll send her there to try and heal. They can work with her far better than any other kind of doctors. She'll be restored to you, Beau, if it's within my power."

"You were angry at her for her part in Abel's death."

"I was, yes. But I think she and Christophe were probably influenced by the diamond earrings your grandfather gave her. I didn't know about those before. Possibly even by the Grimoire and the Bestiary when they went into the cellar. The items weren't exactly active, yet, but they weren't dormant either. Abel had partially awakened them by handling them so much."

"Do you think they affected Camille and Emmanuel too? And what about the missing diamonds? Don't you think they have to be somewhere inside her house at Ravenwood?"

"We have to find those diamonds. As for the rest, I don't know. Rafe has promised to take Gabriel through the home tomorrow to search. It's possible that Camille and her son were affected by the diamonds, but we may never know. I think it's fairly certain Camille heard the argument at dinner that night between you and your grandfather. And she was obviously waiting on him down there. Sophie said they were surprised by him and that he usually went to bed much earlier, so they must have had an assignation that night. She probably wanted to confront him about leaving her and her son out of his will. I believe he must have lied to her and made her certain promises."

"Then when she saw him injured on the floor…"

"Something snapped, I think. The autopsy report was released by the way. They found the wounds were made by a knife like the ones in your own kitchen. Camille must have brought it down with her. Maybe she had plans to kill him all along."

I pulled Beau close to me to comfort both of us. He looked up at me and smiled. "What will you do with the blood diamonds when they find them?"

"Put them somewhere no one can be hurt by them again. The pieces still have the power to do a great deal of evil. I wonder if Camille knew about the curse?"

Beau sighed. "I guess, like you said, we'll never really know." He let his head fall back against the sofa again. "By the way, what was that you told the detective about going to New York?"

I pulled him over and kissed the tip of his nose. "I told you earlier that I'm never leaving you behind again. From now on, where I go, you go."

"Simple as that, huh?"

"Yes."

"And do I have any say in this?" He arched an eyebrow at me as he slid up onto my lap, straddling me.

"None whatsoever," I said, holding his hips and kissing him until neither of us had breath left to say anything at all.

The End

ABOUT THE AUTHOR

Shannon West lives in the southern United States, and is a lover and avid reader of M/M romances. Shannon began writing gay romance a few years ago, and now has over ninety short stories, novellas, and novels to her credit. Her stories have been translated into French, Italian, and even one Japanese Yaoi. Her favorite genre is paranormal and most of her characters don't get really interesting to her until they grow a tail. Shannon loves men and everything about them, and writes Romance (with a capital R) unashamedly and unabashedly. She believes, in the words of Helen Steiner Rice that "love is the answer that everyone seeks, love is the language that every heart speaks." But she also believes wholeheartedly in the words of Woody Allen, that love may be the answer, but "while you're waiting for that answer, sex raises some pretty interesting questions." Shannon mostly spends her days at the keyboard, ably assisted by her cats, Scarlett and Taz, and eluding housework, which stalks her relentlessly.

Painted Hearts Publishing

Painted Hearts Publishing has an exclusive group of talented writers. We publish stories that range from historical to fantasy, sci-fi to contemporary, erotic to sweet. Our authors present high quality stories full of romance, desire, and sometimes graphic moments that are both entertaining and sensual. At the heart of all our stories is romance, and we are firm believers in a world where happily ever afters do exist.

We invite you to visit us at www.paintedheartspublishing.com.

Made in the USA
Columbia, SC
23 September 2019